PETER WHALLEY

ROBBERS

Walker and Company
New York

ROBBERS

First published in the United States of America
in 1987 by the Walker Publishing Company, Inc.

Library of Congress Cataloging-in-Publication Data

Whalley, Peter, 1946–
    Robbers.

    I. Title.
PR6073.H35R6 1987   823'.914   87-14796
ISBN 0-8027-0997-4

Printed in the United States of America

10 9 8 7 6 5 4 3 2 1

I

Miranda Street in Victoria, once a parade of fashionable shops, now paraded the distinctly unfashionable: plumbers, mini-cabs, second-hand books, spare parts for vacuum-cleaners.

Number 21 housed a photographic studio on the second floor, an accommodation agency on the first and a drinking-cum-gambling club in the basement. There was a common entrance at street level but only those in the know – and not in search of bedsitters or passport photos – would have thought to follow the rickety-looking steps downwards to where a door with a peep-hole in it was marked 'Members Only'.

Les Pinfield, a tall, thin-faced man in a leather jacket and open-necked shirt, was not only in the know but in search of a leisurely afternoon's gambling and so trotted down the stairs and knocked on the door. An eye was applied to the peep-hole and Les was admitted.

Inside were a dozen assorted patrons including a couple of tarts and an ex-CID officer. Les nodded to the room in general and ordered a light ale from the swarthy-looking young man who doubled as doorman and barman and was also probably responsible for the posters of Maltese fishing-villages that were sellotaped to the walls by way of decoration.

As Les sipped at his drink, there was another knock at the door, then a small altercation to which he paid no attention until the swarthy young man approached him.

'Somebody here says he knows you.'

Les, who knew a lot of people, went to have a look. 'Oh,' he said. 'Yes.'

Detecting a lack of enthusiasm – even a note of fear – the swarthy young man looked questioningly at Les.

'You're going to sign him in?'

Les managed a slightly sickly grin. 'Sure.'

His guest was admitted and ordered a scotch-and-soda for which Les insisted on paying. The signing-in for which he'd expressed himself willing was never completed; it was enough that he'd offered.

They stood together at the bar, the guest glancing round at the décor and the clientele. Although the newcomer and Les the regular, he already seemed the more at ease.

'You got anything for me yet?' he asked quietly.

'Oh, come on,' protested Les.

'Come on what?'

'Well, not here. I didn't know I'd be seeing you, did I?'

'Sorry if it was a bit of a shock. Only I like to keep tabs on my investment, you know what I mean?'

'I'll see you right,' muttered Les. 'No call for this.'

'I'm glad to hear it.' His guest indicated their surroundings. 'Bit down-market for you is this, isn't it? I mean, the money you must have.'

Les gave a short laugh. There was a pause during which he seemed to grow more uncomfortable.

'Just going for a pee,' he said. 'Back in a tick.'

There was another door at the far end of the basement marked 'Toilets' and 'Fire Exit'. Les put down his glass and headed for it, not hurrying, exchanging the odd word on the way.

His guest watched him go then shook his head sadly, as if bemoaning some weakness or foolishness in one who should know better.

Once out through the door, Les's casual progress

changed abruptly into a frantic charge that took him down the narrow corridor, past the toilets and up the steps at the end where he had to push past sacks of rubbish and crates of empties. At the top of the steps was a door bolted on the inside which was easily opened and which let him out into a walled yard. The door to the street was padlocked and wouldn't budge. With nothing else for it, he reached up, grabbed the top of the wall and, careless of damage to shoes or clothes, hauled himself on to it.

Beyond was a narrow street with not a soul to be seen. Les dropped on to the pavement, decided on his direction and set off at a brisk walk that was almost a run.

At the end of the street was a busier road where he slowed slightly. He was sweating and out of breath. He needed to find a taxi. Urgently. Looking up and down the road for one, and looking behind for signs of pursuit, he kept bumping into people and having to side-step them with muttered apologies.

The taxis that passed were all taken. He came to a junction, saw a tube-station sign and, on impulse, hurried towards it.

'East Ham,' he said, pushing a fiver at the booking-clerk. Then wondered whether he'd done the right thing, finding the escalators and corridors below quieter than he'd expected. It was mid-afternoon, between rush-hours and with the trains less frequent. He cursed himself. Stupid to have fled the basement club then to have plunged himself back down into this maze where there'd be precious little chance of escape if his pursuer arrived before the train did. Still, he was committed now and stood on the platform willing the indicator to announce his train. Or any train come to that.

He had to get home. Where there was an American-made hand-gun with twelve rounds of ammunition. It was in a secret compartment he'd built into the fitted bedroom furniture his wife had nagged him into installing five years earlier. He'd been minding the gun for a friend when the friend had been killed in a car accident and so he'd kept it, never seeing himself as using it but liking the idea that it was there just in case. In case of times like this.

Though he still couldn't see himself using it, at least with it in his pocket he'd be able to make a stand against that murderous bastard who'd been quietly pursuing him for three days now.

The first train was for Upminster, which would do him nicely. There was a sickening moment, as it emerged from the tunnel, when he thought he caught a glimpse of his enemy along the platform. But no. Just someone in a similar coat.

He got onto the train and remained by the doors, looking out, until they closed. Still no sign of pursuit. He sank back onto a seat, his heart thumping. He was out of condition, years out.

Above him, a map of the London Underground showed eighteen stations to East Ham. Say two minutes a station – that'd mean thirty-six minutes. Three-quarters of an hour and he'd be home and dry.

A league-table of the other London underground – the one that ran so much more than just trains – might have placed Les Pinfield somewhere in the lower reaches of the Third Division, a small-time villain and life-long thief, once specialising in break-ins and mail-bag snatches, now semi-retired, more likely to be grafting for one of the big boys than setting up jobs of his own. It'd been an unspectacular career – with one exception – during which he'd made the acquaintance of both police and major villains without either side ever becoming too concerned about him. Only once had he come badly unstuck when he'd made up the number for a doomed-from-the-start supermarket caper. The police had been tipped off; Les had been caught trying to stuff his nylon mask and pickaxe handle into a waste-paper bin and had got three years.

Oddly enough, it was his one big success that'd led to his present problems and left him sweating with fear and itching to light up a cigarette despite the No Smoking notices. It'd been a big wages snatch. For which no-one had ever been copped and away from which they'd all walked with over fifty grand apiece. It'd been front-page headlines for a day and talk of the town for a month. For a while Les had lived like a king, believing his troubles were over.

Now here he was scared witless and knee-deep in debt.

Where had it gone, all that money? A question he'd had good cause to ponder on these last few days. Well, cars. He'd had three or four expensive motors. And women? Well, hardly. Not unless you counted the wife, Paula, who could spend money faster than the Royal Mint could produce it. Certainly faster than he could.

Three stations to go. Still on edge, he got up, walked the length of the compartment and sat down again.

Even his nerve seemed to have deserted him. And that was the one thing he'd prided himself on. That he'd never bottled out, never cried off at the last minute or been unable to go through with a job. He might not have been all that successful but he had kept his self-respect. Until now. Maybe at forty-three he was getting old.

The gun. That was what he needed. After all, he'd never professed to be a man of violence. Never been employed as muscle. The gun would be the equaliser. It'd give him the backing he needed to get this sorted once and for all.

East Ham came at last. He hurried off the train and

was first up the escalator. The fresh air and the feeling of being above ground again calmed him. He even paused to buy a newspaper, proof to himself that he'd stopped running. He was simply on his way home, though somewhat earlier than planned.

He came to his road with its modest semis, deserted at this time of a September afternoon with just a few parked cars and the distant chimes of an ice-cream van.

So that he heard the footsteps behind him clearly enough. There might have been time for another escape had he turned then. But he didn't. For a few vital seconds he couldn't bring himself to look round, hoping – yet with no real hope – that it wouldn't be him at all but would be somebody else, one of his neighbours in a hurry.

Then, finally looking when it was too late, he couldn't fool himself any longer. He gave a grunt of fear and started to run. But the other man, already in motion, was upon him. There was a click and the sprung blade of a knife appeared. 'No, please,' Les pleaded and put up his arms, wincing against the blow even before it was delivered.

His assailant had stepped away before Les felt that pain that was like an intense heat and told him he'd been stabbed. The handle of the knife protruding from the front of his shirt told him the same thing. Yet he still hoped it wouldn't mean he was dying.

He fell to his knees. It was like being drunk was this dying, like being exhausted. Though with a mess of sticky blood that covered his hands. He heard the footsteps going away now, felt them through the pavement on which his head was resting.

His last thought was that the other man must have caught a taxi. It seemed monstrous that life and death should turn on the chance movements of traffic. Somehow there should have been more to it.

II

Process-serving was something Clifford Humphries, founder, proprietor and moving-spirit of the Coronet Private Investigation Agency (Bethnal Green), could do standing on his head. It was simple and straightforward, and the bread-and-butter operation of most private detective agencies. It meant handing over a legal document – which might be a writ, a summons, a bankruptcy notice or any one of a dozen other bits of paper. You handed it over, said good-day and submitted an expenses claim to the solicitor who'd issued it. In the case of the Coronet Private Investigation Agency this was invariably Samuels, Jessop and King of Bethnal Green.

Problems only arose when the recipient took umbrage and refused to accept whatever he was being given. In which case the process-server simply touched him with the document and let it fall. Further and more serious problems arose if the recipient then chose to turn violent, knocking hell out of the innocent process-server who might protest in vain that he was only doing his job.

Twenty-odd years' experience had taught Clifford Humphries to anticipate these problems and take somebody handy along with him. Currently that somebody was Harry Sommers, ex-boxer, ex-most things, who was employed by the Coronet Private Investigation Agency on what might best be called a self-employed and occasional basis.

11

This particular morning Clifford Humphries had invited Harry along to assist in the serving of a bankrupty notice to a Mr Douglas Luke Palmer, scrap-metal dealer and local hard man. The address – flat 92, Mercury House, Fairfields – meant the top floor of a tower-block on the largest council estate in London's East End. As if that wasn't enough, the lifts were out of order.

However, duty called, and Clifford Humphries and Harry Sommers began the slow ascent. Clifford Humphries was a squat, stocky figure, with heavy sideboards to compensate for his baldness. Harry Sommers was taller, hairier and, at little more than half the other man's age, considerably fitter.

By the time they reached halfway, Clifford was needing a rest on every landing. Reaching the top at last, he barely had strength left to press the bell of flat 92.

Mr Palmer answered the door wearing only his underpants. It was an attire that displayed to the full his protruding beer-gut and the tattoos of snakes that ran the length of each arm.

'Mr Douglas Palmer?' gasped Clifford, following the procedure laid down.

'That's me, yes. And who're you?'

'I've been instructed to deliver this to you personally.'

He held out the document. Duggie Palmer hesitated a moment, then took it.

'Thanks.'

'A pleasure. Good-day then.'

'Hang about,' said Duggie.

Harry, who up to then had been keeping in the background, took a warning step forward. Then found he wasn't needed.

'How about a cup of tea? You must be knackered after all them steps.'

'No, thank you,' said Clifford. 'Got to be off.'

'Suit yourself,' said Duggie Palmer cheerfully. 'Good luck, then.'

He closed the door, leaving them to begin their descent.

'Can't tell, can you?' chuckled Harry. 'Everybody has their good days.'

'He probably doesn't realise yet what he's been given,' said Clifford sourly. He seemed put out that it'd all been so easy. Perhaps it was the unnecessary expenditure involved in Harry's fee that irked him.

They trudged downwards. Odd cooking smells floated past; music and raised voices came and went.

'Slow down,' pleaded Clifford.

Harry saw to his consternation that the older man really was suffering.

'Sorry,' he said. 'Do you want me to give you a hand?'

'No. Just stop leaping about like a bleeding gazelle, that's all.'

They came down more slowly and finally reached the litter-strewn hallway where the defunct lifts were parked with their doors open. There were seats there. Clifford dropped onto one with a long groan of relief that ended with a grunt of pain. Harry looked at him anxiously.

'You all right?'

There was no answer. Clifford was bent over, hugging his chest and gasping.

Harry squatted beside him. 'What is it?' But, whatever it was, Clifford couldn't tell him. He could manage no more than a desperate, agonised look that left Harry in no doubt it was serious. 'I'll get some help.'

He dashed back up to the first floor, banging on doors. One finally opened and a suspicious face peered out.

'I need a phone,' said Harry. 'It's an emergency.'

13

He was directed upwards to number 12, where there was no answer, but number 13, who came to see what all the noise was about, suggested he tried number 21 and there at last he was able to dial 999 and answer 'Ambulance' to the operator's enquiry.

By the time he got back to Clifford a group of sympathetic housewives and curious, gawping children had gathered around him.

'Ambulance's on its way,' he announced.

'There's no need,' Clifford protested weakly. 'The pain's going. I'll be all right.'

'He doesn't look it,' commented one of the women.

'You just stay there,' said Harry. 'You might as well have a ride in the ambulance now it's coming.'

'Well, let me get outside,' insisted Clifford. 'A bit of fresh air's all I need.'

Unable to prevent him, Harry took his arm as he stumbled forward. The sightseers parted to let them through and they moved slowly into the open where Clifford leaned against the wall, took out a spotted handkerchief and mopped his brow.

The ambulance arrived, with sirens and lights going that attracted even more attention so that the windows of the tower-block were lined by spectators to watch Clifford being loaded in by two brisk, young ambulancemen who brushed aside his claims that he could walk.

Just in time Harry remembered to ask for the keys to the car. Clifford, with an oxygen mask being strapped across his face, said nothing but one of his hands fished in a pocket and produced a bunch of keys that Harry caught before they hit the floor.

The ambulance went blazing up to the Casualty entrance to the hospital, leaving Harry to find the nearest car-park which turned out to be a quarter of a mile away. By the time he got back to Casualty and made known who he was and what he was doing there, Clifford had been whisked through admission procedures and on to Intensive Care. Harry was directed to a row of stacking-chairs outside the ward and asked to wait.

With time to think, he began to wonder whether he shouldn't have been doing something more than just waiting. Should he be informing somebody of what had happened? Like Clifford's wife for instance. And then Yvonne back at the office.

Or would Clifford himself have already seen to that? After all, he'd been fully conscious and insisting he was feeling better when the ambulance had arrived. Harry decided to give it a quarter of an hour. He still half-expected Clifford, fully-recovered, to come sailing out of the ward to give him a rollicking for landing him in the arms of the National Health when all he'd needed was to get his breath back.

When the doors to the ward did finally open, it was for an Indian doctor in a flapping white coat. Solemn-faced, he came up to Harry and perched on the chair beside him.

'Were you a relative of Mr Humphries?'

Harry was shaking his head and saying no before the past tense registered.

'What, you don't mean . . .'

The doctor nodded. 'I'm afraid Mr Humphries passed away ten minutes ago.'

'I don't believe it,' said Harry, stunned.

'I'm afraid it's true. He had a major coronary. A heart attack. There was nothing anyone could have done. It was all over very quickly. Sister is informing his wife at the moment. I don't know if there is anyone else you think should be told.'

He used Clifford's car to drive back to the office. Isabelle, Clifford's wife and now widow, would be

15

arriving in her own car so there seemed no point in leaving the dead man's vehicle in the hospital car-park. And he'd no wish to hang around and meet Isabelle whom he'd found difficult the odd time he'd come across her in the past and who was sure to be more so under present circumstances. Besides, somebody had to go and tell Yvonne in the office. Find out what Clifford's appointments were and set about cancelling them. Set about closing down the whole business as like as not.

Harry felt a real sadness at his employer's death. Clifford might have been mean – well, he *was* mean, no two ways about it – but he'd been likeable and good company, full of stories about his experiences in his dubious trade. Before becoming a private detective, he'd been a guard on the railways and took a perverse pride in the way he'd set up the business with no previous experience of police or legal work.

'What I did,' he told Harry more than once, 'I looked round and asked myself which of the professions could I get into without having a single qualification to my name. And the answer was – none. 'Cept for this one, private investigation. Which anybody can set up in tomorrow if he likes. Mind you, it's another thing to make a go of it.'

Which Harry didn't doubt. And Clifford had certainly made a go of it. Until now, at the age of fifty-nine, he wasn't in a position to make a go of anything any more. The Coronet Private Investigation Agency was abruptly reduced to Yvonne behind her desk and Harry himself – part-time muscle and aide-de-camp. A poor memorial to the energetic little cockney who'd surely deserved his retirement and a few years of pension.

And all because the bloody lifts hadn't been working. Harry slammed the car door angrily. He'd like to meet the equable Duggie Palmer again and tell him what he thought of his bankruptcy notice, the serving of which had cost Clifford Humphries his life.

The Agency operated from a pair of adjoining offices conveniently near to Messrs Samuel, Jessop and King and, less conveniently, above a dry-cleaners so that the odour of carbon-tetrachloride invested the premises with a kind of ascetic reek.

It also clung to the person of Yvonne who occupied one of the offices and who answered the phone, dealt with clients and made the tea, as well as doing the cleaning and the occasional spot of redecorating. She was a plump, plain woman, pushing forty and unmarried. She'd worked for the Agency for many years and, if she wasn't quite worth her weight in gold – which would have been a king's ransom – she was a valued employee, quite capable of solving the odd case of, say, tracing a missing person which could be managed by telephone off her own bat.

Harry knew she'd be upset by Clifford's sudden death and was at pains to break it to her gently.

'Something's happened to Clifford – Mr Humphries. I'm afraid it's bad news.' She stared at him, openmouthed. 'He's had a heart attack. He was taken to hospital but, well, it was no good I'm afraid and he . . . he's passed away.'

She gave a little cry of despair and then collapsed into uncontrollable sobbing. Harry watched in alarm: he certainly hadn't been prepared for this. She beat on the desk-top with her podgy fists.

'Oh no, no! He can't have died. He can't!'

'I'm sorry,' said Harry. 'But he has, yes. I know it's a shame but . . .'

'It's awful! It's the end of the world!'

'Well now, come on . . .'

'If Clifford's dead then I might as well be dead as well.'

17

And she relapsed into sobbing. Great, heaving spasms of grief that shook her whole body and made further communication impossible. Harry, bemused, patted her hand and then sat waiting, not knowing what to do for the best. He'd been upset himself at his employer's abrupt demise. But this was real grief he was seeing before him, intense and passionate. It was hard to believe that Yvonne had such emotion within her or that Clifford could have been the man to bring it out.

At the first sign that her sobs might be subsiding, Harry quickly offered a handkerchief and said, hoping to distract her into some sort of action: 'I think we'd better try and sort out who should be told. Of course his wife already knows.'

Which, as it turned out, only made things worse.

'That bitch,' snarled Yvonne. 'She would have to know first, wouldn't she!'

'Well,' said Harry cautiously, 'she was his wife.'

Yvonne looked him in the face. Her desperate state made her words impossible to doubt.

'She might have been his wife. But he loved me. I was his mistress.'

'I, er . . . I see,' said Harry.

'For seven years he loved me. He might have lived with her but he never touched her, not during that time. I was the one he loved.'

Harry, speechless, could only make a gesture of sympathy.

'I told him he wasn't well,' she muttered, gulping back the tears. 'I told him he should have been looking after himself. He used to find breathing difficult after we'd been making love.'

Harry cleared his throat. 'Wouldn't it be best if you went home? Took the rest of the day off?'

But no, she wasn't having any of that.

'He'd want us to carry on. Somebody's got to.'

18

'Carry on?' echoed Harry hopelessly. 'But how can we?'

Yvonne gave an enormous sniff, reached for her desk diary and opened it. Her tears dropped onto its pages as she read.

'Well, you've got the school run this afternoon. You can still do that.'

He shrugged. 'OK.'

He could still do the school run, yes, but not much else. After that Yvonne would have to face up to realities: Clifford Humphries had not only been her lover; he'd also been the Coronet Private Investigation Agency. Without him, it'd be lucky to stay open till the end of the week.

Jade Grodzinski was thirteen-and-a-half, had her hair in blonde ringlets and wore a brace on her teeth. She was a day pupil at Fisher's School, an independent school for young ladies established in 1827 within the ancient boundaries of the City of Westminster. She was also the daughter of Billy Grodzinski, East End racketeer and leading importer of pornographic videos and magazines. It was Billy's determined wish his daughter should grow up a young lady – and sod the expense.

However, since a small fracas with a rival organisation in the summer he'd become obsessive about security for himself and his family. One result was that for the autumn term Jade was to be chauffeured to and from school. And not by one of Billy's own minders either. The appearance of one of those gorillas outside the school gates might well have upset the delicate sensibilities of that establishment. Instead, a private detective was hired for the purpose. Billy had contacted Clifford Humphries, whom he'd used before when wanting to keep things kosher-looking. Which was why twice a day Harry, in a Jag supplied by Mr

Grodzinski, made the journey from Woodford to Westminster, first to deliver Jade from home to school, then to collect and return her.

Now, even with Clifford in the hospital morgue, life went on and, with it, the chauffeuring of Jade Grodzinski. Harry arrived punctually and parked in his usual spot outside the school gates.

Truth to tell, he'd found the job oddly nostalgic. Hearing the distant bell for the end of lessons and seeing the first uniformed figures appear took him back to his own schooldays when, to the amazement and even disapproval of his family, he'd passed the eleven-plus and gone to the local grammar school. With good reason his mother always called it the worst thing that could have happened to him, setting him firmly on course for a life of petty crime. The kids in his neighbourhood mocked his fancy uniform; the kids at his new school mocked his common accent. He couldn't win, except with his fists and by going in for displays of bravado – stealing from Woolworths, jumping the railway tracks, beating up prefects – to prove he hadn't gone soft. He and the grammar school eventually parted company when he was fifteen and was expelled for lacing the staff-room tea with a strong laxative. Too late though to return to being one of the lads. The stigma of his eleven-plus success stuck with him. He'd also picked up the habit of reading, which he furtively continued, stealing books from the local library. When he was eventually caught, the worst thing wasn't the appearance before the magistrates or the belting from his father but his mates' scorn when they learnt it was books he'd been pinching and not fags or booze.

When his two brothers got good jobs on the docks, he remained unemployed until, in desperation, he signed on for three years in the army. At least there he learned to control his temper and even came out as a promising amateur boxer. Never good enough to think about turning pro though, he still had to earn a living and did so precariously, helping out here and there, first as warehouseman or barman, then, as his reliability became known, as bouncer or doorman in one or another of the East End's many pubs and clubs.

It was no way of staying out of bother: there followed two more convictions, for assault and causing an affray, which brought him a total of six months in the nick.

At the age of thirty-two, still living at home with his parents and weary of the feeling there'd be more bother around the next corner, he answered an advert in the local paper, one so discreetly worded he was sure it had to be for an encyclopaedia salesman. The idea of encyclopaedias sounded non-violent and appealed. So it was something of a surprise to find himself faced by Clifford Humphries and being told the vacancy was with the Coronet Private Investigation Agency and not even a full-time job at that – just someone to help out when necessary.

'Of course we have the most rigorous vetting procedures for anyone wishing to be employed here,' Clifford Humphries had solemnly warned him. 'So I'm going to ask you before we go any further – have you ever been in any kind of trouble, either in your youth, or with a past employer or with the police?'

'None at all, sir, no,' said Harry, who had a diabolical record on all three counts.

It wasn't so much an attempt to deceive as to avoid embarrassing the genial Mr Humphries with a recital of Harry's chequered career. The truth would anyway come to light when the Agency did its vetting.

So it was with some surprise he read the letter offering him the job. Mr Humphries, it seemed, had been impressed by his application and the rigorous vetting procedure had shown him to have a spotless record.

Later, of course, he got used to Clifford's methods

which relied more on appearance than substance. Behind his desk, angled to catch the eye of any client sitting opposite, was a framed list of rules and regulations headed 'The Association of British Investigators: Code of Ethics'. Rule number one was: 'To perform all professional duties in accordance with the highest moral principles and never to be guilty of conduct which will bring reproach on the profession of private investigation.'

'Very impressive,' he'd once commented to Yvonne in an idle moment.

'It's meant to be,' she said. 'He's not even a member.'

At first he'd been dismayed by this unorthodox and cavalier approach. Was he any better off with this shoddy, tin-pot Agency than he'd been with his former clubland bosses? Till he began to see that, by and large, Clifford didn't do a bad job. He was trusted by at least one firm of solicitors, through whom he got most of his work; he never over-charged unless the client could afford it; and he took a real pride in his profession.

He told Harry: 'They go to the police; they go to the priest; they go to the social worker. And when all these have failed – then they come to me.'

And on another occasion: 'People pay for private education and they pay for private medicine because they want something better than the State can provide. It's the same reason they come to me and pay for private detection.'

Poor old Clifford. Harry hadn't realised till now how close they'd become in the nine months he'd worked for him. He'd miss him. Not as much as Yvonne would miss him, but he'd miss him all the same.

The car door was opened.

'Oh sorry,' said Harry. 'I didn't see you coming.'

Jade flung her briefcase and school coat into the back of the car and got in beside Harry.

'I don't mind you not opening the door for me,' she

said. 'I'm quite capable of doing that myself.' The brace on her teeth made her slur her *s*'s slightly. 'Anyway you looked as though you were miles away.'

'I was,' admitted Harry. 'Now, wouldn't you like to sit in the back? You know your father prefers it.'

'He's not going to know, is he? No, thank you. I'll stay in the front.'

Harry shrugged. He was paid to drive, not argue. Perhaps he wasn't even paid at all any more. He was about to drive off when Jade surprised him by thrusting an arm across his face, pointing at the school gates.

'Oh look, there's Miss Hanscombe. Give her a wave.'

Harry looked and saw a young woman inside a purple Mini. She looked in their direction and smiled.

'Wave,' ordered Jade.

'You wave.'

She did so, calling, 'Bye, Miss Hanscombe', as the Mini pulled out of the gates and went away down the road. Then she turned to Harry. 'She asked me who you were. She'd seen you waiting for me.'

'And what did you tell her?' said Harry, starting the car.

'I said you were a private detective. She was ever so impressed.'

'I'll bet.' It still seemed a strange label to be wearing – private detective. He didn't quite believe it himself and therefore couldn't really expect anyone else to. Still, it probably had the edge on encyclopaedia salesman. 'And she's one of your teachers, is she?'

'Yes. She teaches us English.'

'Does she, now?'

'She's ever so nice. Do you fancy her?'

'Never you mind.'

'That means you do but you're not telling me.'

Did it? He had to admit she was nice-looking. Or anyway as seen through the windscreen of her Mini she was nice-looking. Which was about the nearest he was likely to get. A young lady teaching English at Fisher's School was unlikely to go a bomb on Harry Sommers, ex-con, ex-heavy and chauffeur to gangster's daughter, even if he had once passed his eleven-plus. Besides, it seemed disrespectful to the memory of his recently departed employer to be fancying anybody at the moment.

Jade had taken out a comic and become engrossed in it so that most of the journey was in silence. For which Harry was grateful.

He thought about Yvonne, transformed in his eyes from the office drudge to the grief-stricken mistress. What lay ahead for her? Her lover gone, with her job soon to follow, and an uphill struggle to find a replacement for either.

They were about five minutes from the Grodzinski home when Jade suddenly waved a hand at some houses they were passing and said airily, 'There was a man killed there yesterday.'

'Was there.'

'He was stabbed. I heard Daddy telling Mummy when they didn't know I was listening. I think it was someone Daddy knew although he didn't seem to know much about why he'd been killed.'

'What a terrible thing to happen.'

'Oh, it's not so terrible. These things happen all the time. You're better off not knowing.'

Harry nodded, not wanting to quarrel with the wordly-wise thirteen-year-old who anyway, as the daughter of Billy Grodzinski, might well be better informed than he was.

'Daddy said it was probably some members of a gang falling out. What do you think?'

'I haven't a clue,' said Harry. 'Not a clue.'

Jade gave a little sniff of disdain and returned to her comic.

III

Clifford Humphries's will was read two weeks later in the offices of Samuel, Jessop and King. For the most part it was straightforward enough. The bulk of his estate he left to his beloved wife, Isabelle, barring a sum of two hundred pounds which went to a second cousin in Perth and another two hundred for the Railwaymen's Benevolent Fund.

The Coronet Private Investigation Agency he left lock, stock and barrel to Miss Yvonne Robinson.

Yvonne burst into tears and had to be escorted from the room.

Isabelle, the beloved wife, sat stony-faced. There was a feeling of apprehension: this was a lady who wasn't accustomed to taking anything lying down. However, being no fool and a well-provided-for widow, she decided on this occasion to cut her losses.

'Poor girl,' she said icily. 'She obviously expected more.'

'You won't be wanting to contest it, then?' asked Mr Samuel, the senior partner who'd handled the estate personally in recognition of his firm's long association with the deceased.

'Of course not. I'm just sorry that Clifford – God rest his soul – hadn't been a little more considerate. Obviously he knew I wouldn't want the dreadful business so now he's gone and lumbered her with it. I suppose the best she can hope for is to sell the fixtures and fittings.'

★   ★   ★

Yvonne, though, had other ideas. She explained them to Harry the following day when, recovered from her ordeal, she met him in the tetrachloride-scented office.

'Oh no,' he said. 'I can't. I mean we couldn't.'

'Of course we could,' she insisted. 'Between us we could keep this Agency going. I know all of Clifford's contacts and his ways of working. And he always thought very highly of you.'

Harry, who found it difficult to imagine why, still demurred.

'I've got a prison record.'

'Only a little one.'

'Nobody's going to trust me.'

'People will trust a man who acts as though he expects to be trusted,' said Yvonne firmly. He knew from her tone she was quoting Clifford. 'And anyway they'll never know about your prison record.'

Surely there were other, more fundamental objections.

'But I don't know anything about the business,' he said, finding one at last.

'Of course you do. You worked with him for long enough.'

'Nine months.'

'Yes. And don't forget that Clifford knew nothing about it when he started. At least you'll have me to help.'

Harry sighed and shook his head. As much as with Yvonne, he was arguing with that part of himself that told him not to be a fool and to grasp the chance being offered. Would he be taking advantage of Yvonne or would she of him? Perhaps neither. She might have been offering a half-share but only because the whole share was worthless without him.

'We'll be partners,' she urged. 'It's a good business. You know how much Clifford left.'

He did, and had been as surprised as anybody else.

Clearly there was money to be made, working night and day as Clifford had done.

'I'm a villain,' he said quietly. 'I'm known as one. Oh, nothing big-time but I'm known all the same. And Clifford wasn't.'

'Good.'

'What?'

'I said good. It means you know what's what and it means people won't mess you about.'

'The police might.'

'Not if we do things by the book. And I'll see to that.' Then she added: 'Clifford trusted you.'

It was a difficult appeal to resist. After all, he'd been looking for worthwhile employment from the age of fifteen and now had come this gift-horse of a rare kind, offering occupation, income and status. Not the kind of status to interest, say, a teacher of English at Fisher's School but at least he might start pulling a better class of bird than the ones he currently met in the pubs and clubs where he'd worked and who fell at his feet mainly because they were tanked up on gin-and-orange.

'Well,' he said slowly, 'if I was to say yes . . .'

'Yes?'

'I mean it'd only be for like a trial period. See whether we could make a go of it.'

'Oh, Harry,' she said, tears shining in her eyes.

'All right,' he said, though still with misgivings, 'it's a deal.'

They shook hands. Then he saw to his alarm that she was crying.

'Don't worry,' she gulped. 'This'll be the last time you'll see me like this. After today it'll be back to business.'

It was, though, a business severely curtailed by Clifford's death. Most of the cases on the books somehow evaporated once they heard that the man to whom

27

they'd entrusted their innermost secrets had been indiscreet enough to go and die on them. Even Samuel, Jessop and King went through a period of doubt and put little work in the way of the new management.

Then, whether coincidence or not, Billy Grodzinski decided that his precious daughter could use the tube like everybody else and that her chauffeuring could stop at the end of the week.

'They don't trust us any more,' said Harry gloomily, having just received his instructions that today was to be the last for the school run.

'Don't be silly,' said Yvonne. 'We'll get new cases. It'll just take time, that's all.'

'What new cases?'

'Well, there's a gentleman rung for an appointment this afternoon. I said you could see him after you got back from taking Jade home. He seemed to think you'd know him.'

'What's his name?'

'It's a Mr Phil Holliday.'

It rang a bell but he couldn't place it.

'Did he say what it was about?'

'We would never ask that over the telephone.'

He nodded, accepting the mild reprimand.

'But he did say expense was no object.'

'Good.'

'Mind you, a lot of them say that to start with. It's when they get the bill they change their tune.'

Harry shrugged and looked at his watch. They'd received a commission – a small commission – from Samuel, Jessop and King to serve a couple of writs. No slip-ups there otherwise they'd really be out on their ears.

'Well, I'll certainly see him,' he said. 'Still can't think where I know him from though.'

He was about to leave when Yvonne, blushing

slightly, asked, 'Would you think me a terrible flirt if I told you something?'

It was a difficult question to answer. 'Not, er . . . no.'

'Only I've started seeing my Chinese boy-friend again.'

'Yes . . .?'

'Well, it's awful really. But before Clifford died – when he and I were lovers – well, actually I was seeing somebody else as well. And now I've started seeing him again, this other person. I don't think that's too awful, do you? I mean life has to go on, hasn't it?'

'It has,' said Harry, feeling punch-drunk. So Yvonne had not only been Clifford's mistress – she'd been Clifford's two-timing mistress. And now for some reason she seemed to need his blessing for passion to recommence. 'No, I'm sure that, you know . . . you're doing the right thing.'

'Oh, thank you,' she said. 'I knew you'd understand. And he's a marvellous person. Just a bit small, that's all.'

The girls of Fisher's School came straggling out singly or in groups, older ones already looking dangerously like young ladies, younger ones, with displaced ribbons and falling socks, looking like school-kids everywhere.

Waiting in his usual spot, Harry wasn't sorry it was for the last time. The routine had become boring and the nostalgia kick long since worn off.

Jade came out of the school building and waved to him. He waved back, then suffered a small embarrassment on seeing that what he'd taken to be a schoolfriend standing next to Jade was, in fact, Miss Hanscombe, her English teacher. She gave a smile in Harry's direction that made him fear she'd misinterpreted the wave as aimed at her. Then they parted and Jade came rushing across to the Jag.

'Hello,' she said, climbing in. 'I'm sorry you're

getting the sack.'

'It was never a job for life,' said Harry. 'But it's nice of you to be sorry.'

'Still, I'm sure you'll get other work. There's lots more of it about than people think.'

'Really.'

'Yes, and I could always give you a reference if you needed one.' Then: 'Why aren't we going?'

'Because I'm not ready yet.'

'You look ready to me.'

'Well, I'm not.'

She gave up on him and started fiddling with the radio. Harry turned to look out of his side-window. He knew what he'd suddenly decided was crazy. Perhaps as much as anything he'd been inspired by the example of Yvonne whose own love-life seemed to defy all the odds.

'We're not going to sit here all night, are we?' enquired Jade impatiently.

'No,' he said, seeing what he'd been waiting for. He'd already provided himself with paper and pencil and now used both to make a note.

'What're you writing?'

'Nothing to do with you,' he said, pushing the paper into his pocket before she could get a look at it.

'You don't have to be rude to me just because it's your last day.'

'Sorry,' he said, and started the car.

'Mr Holliday's already here. He's waiting in your office,' said Yvonne as he came in, having safely delivered Jade to the bosom of her family.

'Has he said what it's about?'

'I didn't ask him.'

'Oh no. Course not. And look . . .' He hesitated. They might be partners but he still hadn't shaken off the

30

habit of looking to her for instructions and now felt uneasy about the liberty he was about to take. 'We do have a contact for tracing car numbers, don't we?'

She gave a quick glance towards the other office where Mr Holliday waited – it was a warning to keep his voice down – then admitted, 'Yes. Well, I suppose so anyway. It was a police contact of Clifford's but I suppose he'll still help us if we keep paying him.'

'How much is that?' asked Harry out of interest.

'Ten pounds a time.'

'Oh. So if I give you a car number you can get me the name and address of the owner?'

'I can try.'

He handed her the piece of paper. She looked at it and then asked the question he'd been hoping she wouldn't.

'Is this for a job?'

'Not exactly, no. It's more sort of personal.' Then, before she could follow that up, he said, 'Anyway, better not keep a client waiting, had I?' And walked away into the other office.

The man waiting for him there was in his early forties, stockily-built running to fat and with dark hair cropped short. It was a face Harry found easier to place than the name had been. Phil Holliday was a regular in one of the clubs in which Harry had worked as bouncer. They'd been on terms of easy acquaintance though hadn't met since Harry had left the club for other things.

Phil Holliday now rose from his chair with hand extended.

'Well. Long time no see.'

'It is. And how're you?'

'Oh, fine. And you aren't doing too badly for yourself by the look of things. Somebody told me you'd gone into this racket. I said what, a good East End boy working for the law!'

31

Harry managed a smile. He still felt uneasy in his new role and didn't need reminding it had its absurd side to it.

'It's not the law exactly.'

'Nearer to it than most of us though.'

Harry offered him a coffee, which he refused, and then seated himself uneasily behind the battered, ancient desk that had been Clifford's for so many years.

'No, it's nice to see you again, Harry,' said Phil. 'Nice to see you getting on.'

'Thanks.'

'But this isn't just social. I mean why I'm here – it's business as well.'

'I gathered.'

'Bloody peculiar business an' all. See, I need help. Christ, do I need help. Only there aren't that many people I can go to. So when I heard you'd turned private eye like – well, I thought, just the man I need.'

He lit a cigarette. Harry waited, still a bit short on the kind of chat that Clifford could turn on to put new clients at their ease.

'First of all though,' said Phil, 'can I take it that everything what I say to you in here is absolutely and strictly confidential?'

'Of course, yes.'

'I have your word on that?'

'You do.'

''Cause what I'm going to tell you – well, you'll know when you hear it – it could land a lot of people in a lot of bother.'

'Everything we do is confidential. It has to be.'

'Course it has, yes. Right then. Well, the problem's this.' He took a breath, then announced: 'I'm being blackmailed. Somebody's trying to nail me for ten thousand pounds.'

Harry hadn't known what to expect but it certainly hadn't been this.

'Blackmail . . .?'

'That's it. Pay-up-or-else job.'

Harry shook his head. New to the business he might have been but, if nothing else, he knew its limitations.

'Look, Phil, I mean most of the work we do it's like bits of jobs. Matrimonial stuff, legal stuff. It sounds like it's the Old Bill you want.'

'Can't. Can't go near the Old Bill with this. No chance.'

'Why not?'

'Ah well, that's what I'm going to tell you.'

The nearest Clifford had ever got to criminal investigation had been working undercover in a warehouse trying to find which of the employees was helping himself to the merchandise. There was no way he'd have touched blackmail with a barge-pole.

'But I don't see as I can help,' insisted Harry.

'Well, listen. Won't do any harm to listen, right?'

Though not too sure about that, Harry let him go on.

'I got a letter. Just came through the post like all the others. In fact I've got it here.' He took a folded envelope from his inside pocket and extracted a single, typewritten piece of notepaper. 'I'll read it to you, shall I?'

'If you like.'

Phil put on a pair of reading-glasses before beginning: 'Dear Mr Holliday. Oh, it's dated last week, OK? And no address. Which isn't all that surprising. Anyway. Dear Mr Holliday. I'm sure I don't need to remind you of your part in the Fleet Television robbery that took place in 1977. What's more, I will be prepared to inform a lot of other people about this unless I receive payment from you of ten thousand pounds. To show that you are willing to pay, put a West Ham United badge sticker in your shop window. I will then write again to tell you how to deliver the money. By the way, in case you have any ideas about doing anything clever, remember what

33

happened to Les Pinfield.' He took off his reading-glasses. 'And that's it.'

'Les Pinfield . . .?'

'Didn't you read about it? He got a knife in his guts. 'Bout three weeks ago it was now. Only twenty yards from his own house, in the middle of the afternoon and he gets a knife in his guts. He was dead when they found him.'

Harry nodded. He'd not only read about it, he'd also had young Jade point out the exact spot on one of their journeys home from school.

So it wasn't only blackmail but murder. All the more difficult to see what earthly use he could ever be. Even with Yvonne as back-up, his resources for mounting an investigation fell well short of what the Met could muster.

'For God's sake, Phil! I can't handle this. You've got to go to the cops.'

'No way. D'you think I haven't thought about going to the cops? If I go to the cops then I get myself and six other people stuck inside for a long time.'

Harry hesitated. He wanted to hear more, to have Phil explain further, but knew that the more he heard the greater was the danger of his being dragged in, like it or not.

'Look, Harry boy, I need help, right? I'm on my knees. I'm begging. And there's nobody else I can go to. Believe me there isn't. And I'm not just asking this as a favour. I'll pay, and I'll pay over the odds.'

'For what though? Just what would you expect me to do?'

'Find out who sent the letter. Who's behind it.'

'Oh, is that all?'

'That's all,' said Phil, missing the sarcasm. 'I'm not asking you to do anything about it. I know you can't arrest nobody nor anything. But just find out who's the bastard behind it.'

It was the plea of a man in desperate straits. Made more difficult to resist by the fact they were short of business. Even of the wrong sort of business.

'Let's just get one thing clear first,' said Harry. 'I'm not making any promises. I've already told you this isn't our sort of thing.'

Phil nodded eagerly. 'Understood. Yes.'

'So. You'd better tell me a bit more about what the hell this is all about.'

Phil glanced round as though still fearful they might be overheard.

'Just between the two of us, right? I mean I'm telling you things now I've kept to myself for eight years and never breathed a word about.'

'I know.'

He lit another cigarette. 'Nineteen-seventy-seven there was eight of us did this robbery. Big job it was. Over half-a-million quid. And that was at 1977 prices.'

'A wages-snatch?'

'Wages, yes. And nobody's ever been done for it. The Old Bill's never had a sniff. And the eight of us that did it, we've never worked together since. In fact, me – I've been on the level, straight as a die.'

'You've got a shop?' said Harry, remembering the instructions in the blackmail letter.

'Newsagents. It was what I did with my share of the money, see. I used it to buy the business.'

'And Les Pinfield, the man who was killed . . .'

Phil nodded, anticipating him. 'He was another of the eight, yes.'

'I see.'

'And he'd got the same sort of letter.'

'How do you know that?' asked Harry, surprised.

'Ah well, Les and me, we've always been mates, right. Go back a long way. And so after he'd been killed

35

I was one of them that went to the funeral and his missus – that I've known for a long time so she knows she can trust me, see – she takes me on one side and she shows me a letter. Very like this that I've shown you. And she tells me that Les has got his letter just a couple of weeks before he was killed.'

'So why didn't she go to the police?'

'Well, why should she? It's not going to do Les any good, is it, and it's going to land the rest of us right in it.'

'You mean you advised her not to?'

'I did, yes,' said Phil, resenting the implication. 'I mean you've seen the inside of the Scrubs as well as I have. There's more trying to get out than there are trying to get in, am I right?'

'Go on.'

'Well, that's it really,' said Phil, mollified. 'I didn't see what more I could do. Till I got a blackmail letter as well and then I started thinking well if I don't do something then I'm going to end up the same way as Les.'

'Did Les offer to pay the money?'

'Dunno. But I'd doubt it. I'd doubt if he had it. He could spend money could Les. Easy come, easy go it was with him. More easy go than come most of the time.'

It was heady stuff, thought Harry, this playing at real detectives. He was intrigued by the story of the eight-year-old robbery with its murderous aftermath and ignored the warning bells in his head that said careful, this is deep water and you're going to regret it.

'Something I don't understand though.'

'What's that, Harry?'

'Even if Les did refuse to pay – or couldn't pay – why should the blackmailer have killed him? Instead of exposing him like he'd threatened to?'

36

'Ah well, I've wondered about that. And what I think is that it could have been one of two things. One was that the blackmailer knew that if he exposed Les then he'd be exposing the rest of us as well. And he didn't want that because then he'd have nobody else he could turn the screws on.'

'You mean his plan was to take ten thou off each of you?'

Phil shrugged. 'Why not? He starts with Les. Now he's trying it on with me. I mean maybe he's already tried it on with some of the others and maybe they've already gone and paid him.'

'You haven't kept in touch with the others?'

'No. That was part of the deal – that we'd just come together for the one job.'

Harry nodded. It was a familiar philosophy, this preference for working with strangers. The less you knew about them, the less they were likely to know about you.

'You said there might have been another reason why Les Pinfield was killed?'

'Did I? Oh yes. What occurred to me was – suppose Les had found out who it was. Found out who'd sent the letter? He'd have to be killed then, wouldn't he?'

'Could be.'

'Or maybe that's just the way this bastard plays it. You don't pay up – you get a knife in your guts. I mean I'd rather not have to find out, thanks all the same.'

'I can see that,' said Harry. 'What I still don't see is what I can do.'

'Oh come on, Harry. Don't let me down now. . . .'

'I said I wasn't promising anything.'

It was a protest that didn't convince even himself any more. Simply by listening he'd promised too much. If he'd really been determined to stay out he shouldn't have let Phil even begin to tell his story.

37

'I know you're not promising anything. I'm not asking you to.'

'So tell me, Phil. Just what the hell is it you think I can do?'

'Like I said. Find out who's behind the letters.'

'How?'

'Well, I dunno. You're the bleeding detective!'

'Private investigator,' Harry patiently corrected.

'Same difference. I mean for one thing you can find out about the other members of the gang. The other six. See whether there's been any more of these blackmail letters. And see how they're fixed for money, that kind of thing. Just go and talk to them.'

'So why pay me to do that? Why not do it yourself?'

'Because suppose it is one of them? Then I'm liable to end up with a knife in my guts the same as what Les did.'

So what about me? thought Harry. I'd be going in for ten quid an hour plus expenses and risking exactly the same.

'Please, Harry. There's nobody else I can ask.'

He was so pathetically in need of help it would have taken more callousness than Harry could muster to turn him down.

'So let's see if I've got this right,' said Harry resignedly. 'There were eight of you on this job.'

'Yes.'

'Nobody else knew the first thing about it.'

'Nobody.'

'Then Les Pinfield gets a letter from somebody who does know about it and who tells him he wants ten thousand quid for keeping his mouth shut. Now what Les says to that we don't know. What we do know is that he ends up dead.'

'And then I get the same letter.'

'Yes. So what you're after is me going round this

38

gang of yours trying to sniff out what's what. Like whether anybody else has received any more letters. Or who might be short of money . . . or whatever.'

'That's it. Absolutely.'

'I still think you'd be better off going to the cops.'

'Well, I'm not going,' said Phil, sticking to his guns now he could see he was winning. 'I've come to you instead.'

Harry got up, left his desk and peered out through the window. It was quite a pleasant day. He could have spent it fishing on the canal instead of acting as father-confessor to a reformed villain. He came back to the desk.

'Well, I suppose you'd better tell me all about this robbery, then. And give me the names of these other six.'

'Will do,' said Phil eagerly. 'Hey, and thanks, Harry. I'm very grateful.'

'You should be.'

'So. Where do you want me to start?'

'I dunno. Wherever you like.'

So Phil started at the beginning.

First I hear of it is one night when I'm out pubbing it and I go in the King Billy that's down off Whitechapel Road and Les Pinfield's there and he says he knows this firm in North London that're doing a big job and do I want to come in on it? Course I'm very doubtful on account I'm for the high-jump if I'm nicked again and who the hell is this firm anyway? But Les is very persistent and he says Ronnie Franks and Tommy Coyle are interested and I know they're good lads so I says well, go on then, what is it? He says it's a pay-roll snatch. I says where? He says Fleet Television. I says oh great, we're all going to be on the telly, are we? But Les says look Phil, don't mess about, are you interested or not? So I says yes and we go to meet Ron and Tommy who just happen to be waiting in another boozer round the corner. Tommy says oh you've persuaded him then, meaning me, but I say hang on, I want to hear a lot more first. So Les says well it's a North London firm, very experienced, very professional, only it's too big a job for them on their own so they want us to go in with 'em. Four of them – four of us. Eight altogether and fair shares for everybody. I say but fair shares of what though? At least half-a-million says Les. So we all go quiet for a minute while we're doing sums in our heads and we all have to admit we quite like the sound of it. But hang on I says. What chance we'll ever get to spend it? Because the wife has just had our second and I'm not looking to do any more bird, not for any amount of money. And there's a general agreement on that. But Les says no sweat, this other firm they all think the same and there's going to be total security. Just the eight of us and nobody else'll have a smell. Nobody inside to be paid off, no drinks for the Old Bill, a very tight operation from start to finish. We have the share-out straight after and then everybody's away. So anyway we agree to a meet with this other firm and so a couple of days later Les takes us in his car to this flat that he says is Frank's, whoever Frank is. It's somewhere in Islington and there are these four blokes there, all strangers to me. Les does the introductions and it turns out that Frank is Frank Metcalf and the other three are Neil Patterson, Vince Jardine and Maurice Scanlon. Which leaves me none the wiser but that's not necessarily a bad thing 'cause who wants to be famous in this game? So we all sit down and it's Frank Metcalf who does most of the talking. He tells us how Vince, who's sitting next to him, has been grafting for Fleet. Scene-shifting I think he says – anyway something legit as a change from thieving. And he's noticed how the money for wages, expenses and what-have-you comes in every Thursday morning. Course it comes in a security van – what doesn't nowadays? – and it's taken in at the front door and then up in a lift and along a corridor to get to the cash office. And this is where this Vince reckons they're vulnerable. Inside the building. And obviously Frank and the other two agree with him. Course we want to know everything. How do they know how much is being carried? What about the security guards – they surely don't just dump the cash inside the front door? How would we get inside the building in the first place? And lots more. 'Cause not only is there our futures riding on this but always when you get a meet between different firms they're both out to show the other how smart they are. But eventually we have to hand it to them. They've gone over all the angles and the more we go on asking, the more they just sit there and go on answering. Till in the end we run out of questions. So Les turns to us and says what do you think? Well Ron and Tommy are dead keen and they're nodding and saying yes and then he looks at me 'cause I've been the one with the doubts right from the start. How about it Phil he says. And now they're all watching me. And I say OK, you're on. And everybody relaxes as though that's the difficult part over and done with and Frank produces a bottle of scotch and we drink a toast. And I think about Margie and the kids and how she'd crucify me if she knew I was at it again but I swear to myself it'll be just the one, the big one that'll set us up. And, say what you like, I've stuck to that, been straight as a die ever since.

IV

After finally saying goodbye to the garrulous Mr
Holliday, Harry took himself for a quick drink which,
in the manner of quick drinks the world over, lasted
until the small hours. Whether he was seeking relief
from listening to Phil Holliday rabbiting on or from the
more general strain of his new role, it left him the next
morning with a jumbo-sized hangover.

On top of which came the memory of what he'd
promised Phil Holliday: that he'd try and trace his
blackmailer and Les Pinfield's murderer. A task that at
the moment felt as far beyond him as swimming the
China Sea.

'I think I've done something I shouldn't,' he confes-
sed to Yvonne.

'You look as though you need a coffee,' she said, and
went to switch on the electric kettle.

'Well yes, but it's not that.'

'Is it to do with that Mr Holliday who came to see
you?'

He nodded. Then wished he hadn't as his head began
throbbing madly.

'What did he want?'

'Well . . .' He hesitated. Could he confide to her
something on which he'd been sworn to secrecy? Not
really up to dealing with the ethics of that, he decided to
play it safe. 'Sorry, but it's like confidential. And for
good reasons.'

'That's all right,' she said, and went on making the

coffee. He couldn't tell whether or not she was offended.

However much he might now regret it, he'd committed himself to at least a token show of investigating this wretched business, if only to prove to Phil that he'd come to the wrong man.

'I need some addresses. Do you think you can find them for me if I give you the names?'

'I can try.'

'I've written them down.'

He placed a sheet of paper on her desk. On it he'd printed in block capitals the names of Phil Holliday's ex-confederates:

TOMMY COYLE
NEIL PATTERSON
RONNIE FRANKS
VINCE JARDINE
FRANK METCALF
MAURICE SCANLON

The address of Les Pinfield's widow he already had. Phil Holliday had given him that as well as promising that he'd ring Paula Pinfield and explain that Harry would be calling that morning.

Yvonne brought him the coffee and said, 'I've got some paracetamols if you want.'

'No, thanks,' said Harry. 'I'll stick to coffee.' Then, out of curiosity he asked, 'These addresses I want – how will you set about tracing them?'

She looked at him and gave a prim, little smile. 'That's my secret. That's confidential as well.'

So she was offended. Well, too bad. He couldn't do much about it at the moment.

'I've got to go,' he said. 'See you later.'

'Would you like this?'

'What?'

43

She tore a page from her note-pad, folded it once and handed it to him.

'That other name and address you wanted. The one to go with the car number.'

'Oh. Yes, thanks.'

Truth to tell, he'd forgotten all about it. Now he waited until he'd made a welcome escape from the office and out into the fresh air before he unfolded the paper and read it. 'Jill Hanscombe,' it said. '48 Ashley Road, Chiswick, London W6.'

The police contact had come up trumps, then, and traced Miss Hanscombe to her lair. It would have been encouraging though to have found she lived somewhere nearer: Chiswick was virtually the other side of London. He couldn't help feeling it was ten quid down the drain. Either he'd never get round to doing anything about it or he'd go knocking on her door and find it answered by her boy-friend. Life was full of little surprises, most of which were of the wrong sort.

Phil Holliday had done his stuff so that Paula Pinfield was ready and waiting for Harry when he turned up at her door. The house gave no clue to her ex-husband's doubtful profession. It was a neat semi, newly painted and surrounded by a neat, tidy garden.

Nor did Paula's own appearance give any indication of her recent bereavement. She was wearing plenty of make-up, a well-fitting silk dress and six-inch heels.

It wasn't, Harry felt sure, a special effort for his benefit. She was the type of woman who dressed each and every day as if the drop of a hat might plunge her into some gay social whirl where she'd want to look her best.

'Won't you come in, Mr Sommers,' she said, showing him through to a lounge that was as meticulously laid out as the outside of the house had suggested it might be. The photographs on display were mainly of Paula herself. One or two were quite startling, showing her much younger and apparently taking part in a beauty contest or some modelling assignment. But at least a couple did feature a tall man by her side, which Harry took to be his first glimpse of the recently deceased Les Pinfield.

'Would you like a cup of tea?'

'I wouldn't mind at all, love, thanks.'

He knew as he spoke that he was breaking one of Clifford's cardinal rules: never accept drinks when working; they get in the way of the interview and then make you want to pee. But then Clifford had probably never had to endure a hangover like this one.

Rather than sit by himself in the lounge, he followed Paula out into the kitchen, which was in mint condition and fitted out from floor to ceiling with microwave, dishwasher, freezer, everything in its place.

'You know why I'm here?' he asked, still feeling awkward in his investigator's role. 'I mean Phil did mention, did he . . .?'

'He did, yes. Do you take sugar?'

'No, thanks. It was terrible what happened to your husband. The way he died.'

'It was.'

'Do you mind talking about it? Answering questions?'

'If I did then I'd be used to it by now. The police asked enough of them.'

'I'll bet they did.'

So, the preliminaries over, he was free to launch into his questions. If only he could think of them.

'This letter your husband got – can you, you know, tell me anything about it?'

'Well, what do you want to know?'

'Did he tell you about it when it first arrived?'

'No.'

'He didn't mention it at all?'

'No.'

'Ah,' said Harry, feeling he'd run into a cul-de-sac.

'The first I knew of it was when I was going through his desk – this was after he'd been killed – I was going through his desk and I found it then.'

'I see. So he didn't sort of, er, express any opinion about who might have sent it?'

'Mr Sommers, he was well beyond expressing any opinions on anything by the time I found it.'

'Yes,' said Harry apologetically. So, OK, it'd been a stupid question. 'But did he seem, you know, worried about anything?'

She gave a small, scornful laugh which he first thought was provoked by his feeble attempts at interrogation. Until she explained: 'Les was always worried about something. Normally about which horses had managed to lose which races.' She passed him his cup of tea. 'Shall we go and sit in the lounge?'

He followed her through and perched on a chintz-covered armchair.

While he was still searching for his next question, she said, 'I believe Phil's got one of those letters himself now. That's why he's been to see you, is it?'

There could be no harm in admitting what she seemed to know already.

'Yes. He wants me to try and find out who's been sending them.'

'And do you think you will?'

'I, er . . . I don't know.' He seemed to have lost the initiative. 'Do you know anything about this robbery your husband was involved in?'

'Which one? There were several.'

'The one referred to in the letter.'

'Nothing that'll help you I'm afraid. I knew when it'd

happened, if only because he seemed to have some money for once in his life.'

'Quite a lot from what I hear.'

For the first time she went onto the defensive.

'Quite a lot, yes. More than all his other ridiculous escapades ever produced.'

'Did he talk about the other people he was working with?'

'No.'

'Never? Not a word?'

She answered him with an assured smile, now back into her stride. 'Mr Sommers, I long since washed my hands of my husband and his crazy schemes. Every one of which was going to make us rich. And look at me now. Do you know what I'm having to do to survive?' Harry shook his head. 'I run a launderette.'

It took some imagining.

'A launderette . . .?' muttered Harry.

'He took a lease on it after that robbery you're talking about. Only the machines are so clapped-out it barely makes enough to pay for itself. And now of course I'm left with it. Filling soap-machines and mopping the floor.'

'It can't be much fun.'

'It's never been much fun, Mr Sommers. Not with Les.'

As he floundered for another question, she gave a little laugh. 'You must think I'm hard,' she said. 'You must have expected I'd be all upset and still shedding tears over him. Well, I've shed a few and there are those who've seen me do it. But you see, Mr Sommers, over the years I've had to learn to be hard and to look after myself. Because there was no way Les was ever going to do it.'

'I see.'

'Oh, I'm not saying he was a bad man. He wasn't.

47

But he was weak. He was a weak man who had big ideas, none of which ever came to anything.'

'Except for this Fleet Television job,' said Harry quickly.

'Oh, that.' She shrugged. 'Yes, I suppose he did all right out of that for a time. But then what sort of life did that give me? Expecting the police night and day. And where the money went to I'll never know.'

Which brought them back to the matter in hand.

'Could some of it have gone to this blackmailer? Did your husband perhaps pay him anything?'

'I don't know. I've really no idea what he did.'

'Can I see the letter?'

'If you like,' she said.

It was on the mantelpiece, lodged beneath a pewter candlestick. She brought it to him.

'Thanks.'

'Dear Mr Pinfield,' he read, 'I'm sure I don't need to remind you of your part in the Fleet Television robbery that took place in 1977. What's more, I will be prepared to inform a lot of other people about this unless I receive payment from you of ten thousand pounds. To show you are willing to pay place a garden gnome in the middle of your lawn. I will then write again to tell you how to deliver the money.'

It was almost identical to the one received by Phil Holliday. Except, of course, for the additional threat that'd been appended to the second letter, the reference to Les's violent end.

'Did he put the gnome in the garden?'

'Not that I was ever aware of.'

'I see.' He gave her the letter back. 'Thanks.'

'Is there anything else?'

Clearly he'd outstayed his welcome. And, anyway, he was getting nowhere fast. He should have spent last night preparing his line of questioning instead of boozing himself into near unconsciousness. He made a final effort.

'Did you know any of these people your husband worked with in the robbery?'

'No.'

'Did he talk to you about them?'

'I've told you, no.'

'But what about Phil Holliday? Surely you knew . . .'

'Oh yes,' she said impatiently. 'I knew Phil. Everybody knew Phil. It didn't mean I knew what they were getting up to together.'

There was one more question, the only one he had thought out in advance.

'I'd like to ask you a small favour, Mrs Pinfield. It's something that would help me a lot.'

'What?'

'When I see these other people your husband worked with – that's if I ever find them – would you mind if I gave the impression that I was working for you? I mean instead of for Mr Holliday?'

'Why on earth should you want to do that?'

'Well, it saves me having to mention the letters. I mean it's natural you want to find out who killed your husband. Now if you thought the police weren't getting anywhere you might have come to me. It just gives me a sort of cover if you see what I mean.'

She clearly wasn't keen. He was sure she'd say no, the way she frowned while thinking about it.

Then she shrugged and said brightly, 'You can say what you like as far as I'm concerned, Mr Sommers. I really don't see the point but I'm the last person to want to stand in your way.'

It was hardly a vote of confidence.

The rest of the day he was engaged on the pointless and boring task of following an insurance broker whose

wife suspected him of infidelity and who'd engaged the
Agency to log his movements at certain times during
the week. What made it particularly pointless and
boring was that the insurance broker didn't make any
movements but spent each day working diligently in his
office.

Harry parked his car in a suitable vantage point and
settled down to a lunch of hamburger and chips and a
consideration of what little Paula Pinfield had been able
to tell him.

He doubted her claims to have known next-to-
nothing about the robbery and nothing at all about the
letter. He'd no specific reason for this, just a general
feeling that here was a woman who'd have kept a sharp
eye on what Les was getting up to.

It also said a lot about her own allegiances that she'd
taken the blackmail letter to Phil Holliday and not to the
police. She might have appeared the model housewife,
serving tea in cups and saucers, but she'd also been the
wife of a professional villain. Her first instinct on
needing help had been to turn, not to the police, the
long-standing enemy, but to her own kind.

Otherwise his interview with her had been a waste of
time. Perhaps it hadn't been well enough planned. The
lesson for him was to do his homework; he was no
smooth-tongued sleuth who could busk his way
through.

After which he fell asleep. It wasn't a recommended
technique for a private investigator on a stake-out. Just
that he was short on sleep from last night, the inside of
the car was warm and he didn't believe the insurance
broker was ever going to stir out of his office in a
thousand years.

Nevertheless it gave him a shock to wake up and
realise an hour and a half had passed. He felt better but
decidedly guilty and took a quick stroll past the

insurance broker's window to check he was still inside. Which, thank God, he was.

An hour later it was time to call it a day. He rang Yvonne from a telephone-box.

'Anything come up?' he asked.

'Samuel, Jessop and King have got something for us for tomorrow. Nothing else though.'

'Have you got anywhere with that list of names I left?'

'I've got three addresses so far. Do you want me to give you them now?'

'No, thanks. Tomorrow'll do. And I'll do my report on this surveillance thing tomorrow, OK? I'm going to get off home now.'

Going home was via a painfully circuitous route. So circuitous as to be mostly in the wrong direction altogether. Then, lo and behold, he was in Chiswick, stopping once to ask directions and ending up in Ashley Road.

Number 48 was easily identified by the purple Mini parked outside. It was a large, Victorian house now sub-let into flats. According to the row of bells on the front door, Miss J. Hanscombe lived in number 5.

The last thing Harry fancied was trying to explain himself over the answer-phone. Checking there was no-one around, he took out a plastic credit-card – which had someone else's name on it and, anyway, was years out of date – and used it to push back the simple Yale lock. A moment later and, still unobserved, he was inside.

That had been the easy part. He still had little idea of what he was going to say to the lady; only that, having come this far, it was something he had to go through with. He found flat 5 and knocked on its door.

When Jill Hanscombe answered it, he was caught off-guard, thrown by the small shock of being suddenly

51

in close confrontation with what had hitherto been a distant figure. She was older than he'd expected – middle thirties? – with straight, blonde hair.

'Yes,' she said.

Her sharp, refined tone nearly had him turning and running there and then.

'I've, er, I've seen you outside school. When I've been picking up Jade Grodzinski.'

'Oh yes.' She relaxed slightly, recognising him. 'You're some sort of private detective.'

Not a bad description he thought.

'I was just sort of passing and I recognised your car outside.'

'Don't tell me I haven't got a tax-disc . . .?'

He smiled at her little joke, feeling tongue-tied and stupid.

'No. Nothing like that.' There was nothing for it but to come clean. 'I just wondered if you'd let me buy you a drink sometime.'

At least she didn't scream. Just smiled and said, 'Well, that's very nice of you.'

'Well, it's a bit of a cheek really.'

'Do you live round here?'

'Not exactly, no. Look, what about tonight? I mean would you, er . . .'

'I'm sorry, I'm busy tonight,' she said.

Oh well, that was it, he thought. It might have been a more polite brush-off than the 'sod off, darling' he'd been used to but it amounted to much the same.

'What a shame. Well anyway, if you ever want a private detective give us a ring, eh.'

And he was actually stepping away when she said, 'But I'm free tomorrow. How would that be?'

It took a moment for it to sink in.

'Oh. Yes . . . great.'

'Did you have anywhere in mind?'

He didn't, no. He was so far off his patch he didn't know anywhere nearby, while the few places he knew up West were probably not the kind she was used to.

'I'll pick you up, shall I?' he said. It'd give him time to scout around and find somewhere.

'All right. If it's not putting you to any trouble.'

He said no, it wasn't and they arranged a time. So eager was he now to get away before she might change her mind that she had to call him back to ask, 'What's your name? You haven't said.'

'Oh, sorry. It's Harry. Harry Sommers.'

'Mine's Jill.'

Just in time he stopped himself saying that, yes, he knew – he'd had her traced through the police computer.

Let me explain about the building. This is Fleet Television,
right. Their main offices down St John's Wood. You go in the
main entrance and it's a big foyer and a desk with a few
security blokes hanging about giving you the once-over and
being very particular about checking everybody's passes unless
I suppose you were Des O'Connor but even then I don't
know, perhaps they ask him for his pass as well. Us they'll
certainly ask. So that's the first thing we're going to need.
Anyhow, once past the security, you come to three lifts, which
are the ones everybody uses, and then further on there's
another one that's like the service lift and this is the one the
money goes up in. Up to the fourth floor where the cash office
is.. Now there's four security guards who come with the money
and stick with it while it's being unloaded from the van. And
then there's Fleet's own people about as well so you'd need like
the entire SAS to try and snatch it then. But once it's in the lift
there's only two of these security guards gets in with it.
Meanwhile on the fourth floor there's another two of Fleet's
own people comes from the cash office to meet 'em. So what we
do is take out these two before the lift arrives. Then when it
does arrive the doors'll open and we'll be standing there, five or
six of us versus two security guards who'll be so flabbergasted
at the reception they're getting they won't know what's
happening till it's all over. Then comes the clever bit. Not that
it's not all clever but this is like the icing on the cake 'cause
what we do then is we get into the lift with the money and we
go down again, not to the foyer which is full of security men
saying hello to Des O'Connor, but down past there to the
bottom floor. Which they call the studio floor on account of
that's where the studios are. I imagine. Anyhow that's where
we come out of the lift with the money and straight out into the
loading-bay at the back of the building where we have two
motors waiting so we can be five miles away before anybody's
any the wiser. Course the timing has to be spot on. And the
other main problem is getting us all inside the building and
getting the motors where they have to be in the loading-bay.

For which we need passes. Now Vince – the bloke that's been working in the place and whose original brainwave it is – he still has his pass that they've given him. And Les says he knows somebody reliable that can copy it. Great, says Frank, get 'em to make us a dozen then we'll have spares in case anybody loses one. And then one night, after it's gone dark, Vince takes Maurice Scanlon and they climb over into the car-park at the back of Fleet and nick a couple of parking-discs from two of the wagons that're out there. Which means we can get the motors in. Two days later Les turns up with a handful of passes. Says his friend found 'em easy as pie to copy. So we all goes into Woollies and takes turns sitting in the automatic photo booth so we've got the pictures we need to stick on the passes. Soon as we've done that we can walk in and out of Fleet Television as if we're Des O'Connor and his backing group.

V

The three addresses Yvonne had come up with were for Tommy Coyle, Neil Patterson and Ronnie Franks. Harry decided to tackle the last one first since it was in the same East London district of Barking as was one of the writs he'd been commissioned to serve that day on behalf of Messrs Samuel, Jessop and King.

Yvonne seemed to have forgiven him for his refusal to confide in her about the Phil Holliday interview.

'You wanted to know how I got the addresses,' she said.

'If you don't mind telling me.'

'Well, it's no great mystery. Those three were dead easy. I just got them from the phone book. The only problem is eliminating identical names.'

'And how do you do that?' said Harry, feeling a show of polite interest was called for.

'Oh, ring each one up, make an excuse and find out something about them.'

'I see,' said Harry, though he didn't – not quite. Since Yvonne knew nothing about the nature of the case, how could she select, say, the most likely T. Coyle from a list of T. Coyles? Had she, after all, been listening in to his interview with Phil Holliday?

It might have been to avoid facing any such query that she hurried on with her explanation.

'Then there's the electoral register, only that can take days to plough your way through. And then there are credit agencies. Though they can usually only trace somebody who's been a bad debtor. And, of course, they charge us for the privilege. Oh, and last of all, if we're really desperate' – she lowered her voice, marking this last bit as Top Secret – 'we do have a contact in the DHSS. Somebody that has access to their computer. But that really is a last resort because it could get us into serious trouble. And it has to be paid for.'

'You shouldn't be telling me this,' joked Harry. 'I used to think it was all magic.'

'Well, there is a bit of that as well,' she said, smiling coyly.

The Ronnie Franks address led him to a block of 1950s council maisonettes. He walked along the first-floor balcony till he found number 15 and rang the bell. However, there was no reply nor any sound of movement from inside. He rang again and waited, then tried peering in through the window but could see no further than a set of yellowing net curtains.

He was turning to leave when he found the narrow balcony all but blocked by a young black woman coming towards him. Behind her was a bespectacled, middle-aged white man.

Harry moved to let them pass but the woman stopped and said challengingly, 'You looking for somebody?'

'I am,' said Harry. 'Ronnie Franks. Do you know him?'

She squinted up at him, suddenly suspicious. 'What d'you want him for?'

'He's a pal of mine.'

'Is he? Well then, you ought to know he won't be in at this time. He'll be down at the car-lot.'

'And which car-lot is that, then?'

Her suspicions increased. 'Are you the police?'

Before Harry could reply, the other man, who'd been hanging back behind her, blurted out, 'I've changed my mind. Sorry.' And he scuttled away, back along the balcony.

'Hey . . .!' she called. 'Hey, come back here!' But he

kept going and disappeared down the steps at the end of the block. 'Oh, shit man,' she said. 'Now look.'

'Sorry,' said Harry. 'And I'm not the police, no.'

'You want to go and tell him that?' she said, meaning her nervous companion.

'I will if I see him,' promised Harry with a smile. At least she seemed able to see the funny side of it and wasn't going to make a scene. He tried again. 'So where is this car-lot?'

'Well, what's your hurry? Now that I'm free and seeing as you aren't the cops why don't you and me have some fun?'

'Sorry, darling,' said Harry. 'Another time, eh. Only it's urgent I find Ronnie.'

'Anybody ever tell you you've got nice eyes?'

Eventually accepting that, nice eyes or not, Harry wasn't interested, she gave him the directions he wanted, even walking part of the way with him. The car-lot was no more than an area of waste-land surrounded by a barbed-wire-topped fence and with a small Portakabin in the middle. The cars were drawn up like covered wagons in a circle around it, each with a sticker across its windscreen on which the words 'Warranty', 'Easy Terms' and 'One Owner' were emblazoned in red.

Harry went up to the open door of the Portakabin. Inside, a man was sitting at a small desk on which was spread an open newspaper and a clutter of papers and cards. He had a thin moustache and springy, dark hair. There was a one-bar electric fire strategically placed by his feet.

'And what can we do for you, squire?'

'Are you Ronnie Franks?'

The other man looked at him, taken aback. 'Depends on who's asking.'

Harry smiled. 'I am,' he said, and stepped inside the makeshift office. He lowered himself onto the only other chair. 'Only I wondered if we might have a chat.'

'What about?' said Ronnie Franks, his defences up.

This time Harry had his opening gambit prepared.

'I'm a private investigator. I'm making enquiries regarding a Mr Les Pinfield on behalf of his wife.'

'You what?'

Ronnie Franks's puzzlement seemed genuine. He also seemed a touch relieved which made Harry wonder who he first thought he might have been. Presumably with a past career as a villain and a present one as a used-car salesman, you tended to be a bit jumpy at the approach of strangers.

He repeated his introduction, then added, 'I believe you once worked with Les Pinfield?'

'What kind of work?'

Though the air of puzzlement had now gone. You've remembered well enough, thought Harry.

'Look, Mr Franks, I'm not the law. All I'm interested in is what Mrs Pinfield wants me to find out about her husband. So anything you tell me it's strictly confidential, OK?'

'Well, I'm glad to hear it. Only I don't happen to know what the hell you're on about.'

'You don't?'

'Not a clue.'

This, Harry felt sure, was a lie. He'd found the right Ronnie Franks, no doubt about that.

'Well, do you mind if I ask you some questions?'

'Don't mind at all. Here, have a drop of coffee while you're doing it.'

He took the top off a vacuum-flask and poured what looked like decent enough coffee into two plastic beakers. Harry was encouraged to find that he seemed glad of the company; perhaps he welcomed the prospect

59

of a battle of wits to liven up the afternoon.

'You knew Les Pinfield, then?'

'I've known a lot of people. Only I've a shocking memory for names. Diabolical.'

'Les Pinfield,' repeated Harry patiently.

'It rings a bell,' Ronnie admitted.

'You know he's been murdered?'

Ronnie nodded. 'I heard something of the sort. I'd have sent a wreath only you never know what conclusions the Old Bill's going to draw, you know what I mean.'

'You worked with him on a big robbery eight years ago.'

'Did I, now?'

'There was you, Les Pinfield, Phil Holliday, Tommy Coyle, Neil Patterson, Vince Jardine, Maurice Scanlon and Frank Metcalf. You did Fleet Television for half-a-million quid.'

It surprised Harry to find he'd got the names of the robbers off by heart. It surprised Ronnie even more.

'Well, you are a clever fella, aren't you? And I suppose you're going to tell me what the weather was like and who scored the winning goal in the Cup Final?'

Harry ignored that. 'Les's missus thinks he was being blackmailed,' he said.

The surprise seemed genuine enough. 'Blackmailed . . .? What, you mean somebody was out to shop him?'

'Yes.'

'Jesus.'

'You haven't had anybody having a go at you?'

'You mean somebody trying to put the arm on me? No. No way.' He seemed affronted by the suggestion. 'Nobody's going to try it on with me, I can promise you that.' Then he added quickly, 'Not that I'm admitting to any of this robbery business, mind. It's a right fairy-tale you've been sold is all that.'

Harry shrugged. 'Wouldn't matter, would it? If somebody else'd heard the same fairy-tale, they still might try and screw you for five thousand quid to keep their mouth shut.'

'Be wasting their time,' muttered Ronnie. But he seemed disconcerted by what he'd been told and stared out of the Portakabin windows as if on the alert for an approaching enemy.

'And that's why Les got done, was it?' he said, turning back to Harry.

'That's what his missus wants to find out.'

'How d'you know it wasn't something else altogether? I mean he was always getting involved in one thing and another was Les.'

'I don't. That's why I've come to see you.'

'Tell me them names again. The ones I'm supposed to have been on this job with.'

Harry obediently recited them. Ronnie smiled.

'And who gave you them?'

'I'm afraid I can't tell you that.'

'And was that all they gave you? Nothing else?'

'What else is there?'

But Ronnie wasn't going to be drawn.

'Well now, you're the one with the stories. Me, I'm just trying to sell motors.'

He might have been shaken but only into an increased caution. Harry had the familiar feeling of getting nowhere fast.

'Was there anybody in the gang had a particular grudge against Les Pinfield? Anybody he didn't get on with?'

Ronnie gave a little laugh. 'My memory again,' he said. 'Like I say, it's diabolical.'

'Mr Franks, I'm not interested in the robbery. You could have done the Bank of England for all I care. I'm only interested in who might have killed Les Pinfield.'

'Well, it wasn't me.'

'I'm not suggesting it was.'

'That's very kind of you.'

'Did anybody else know about the robbery?'

'What robbery's this, then?'

'Oh, come on,' sighed Harry. It might have been diverting entertainment for somebody stuck in a Porta-kabin all day but he'd had enough of it.

'Oh, you mean this story you've got about Fleet Television?'

'That one, yes.'

'Well, if nobody's ever been done for it then I'd say not a lot of people must have known about it. I mean if you was asking for my opinion as like an impartial observer.'

'That's exactly what I am asking. So you don't think anybody else was in the know?'

'I can only think of one,' said Ronnie. 'I mean if this fairy-story's true and these eight people did do the robbery and none of 'em's ever been done for it then it seems to me there can only have been one other person that's got to know about it.'

'And who's that?' asked Harry, his hopes rising.

'You.'

Harry came away from his interview with Ronnie Franks confident that here was a man he wouldn't ever buy a used car from but who had had nothing to do with Les Pinfield being blackmailed and murdered.

Evidence of this was the time he'd taken to get to grips with what Harry had come for: despite his pretence of not remembering anything, much of his surprise had been genuine. Nor had he corrected Harry when Harry had deliberately misquoted the blackmail demand as being for five thousand instead of ten.

He'd been on the defensive certainly, but no more

than was to have been expected. Obviously he was going to box clever when invited to implicate himself in a serious crime.

Only two things had given Harry pause for thought. One had been when, looking back on his way out of the compound, he'd seen Ronnie Franks on the telephone. He might, of course, have been speaking to anyone about anything: he just hoped he'd never find out.

The other had been when Ronnie had pointed out that Harry's own name must be added to the list of those in the know. He hadn't made any more of it than that, but it left Harry uncomfortably aware of how easily he himself might appear in the role of blackmailer. Here he was reminding villains of past crimes and asking about blackmail. It'd be no joke if he were to be misunderstood as making oblique demands of his own.

Trying to put that unsettling thought behind him, he set out on his second doubtful enterprise of the day and headed towards Chiswick where Jill Hanscombe would be waiting.

'I hope you weren't expecting the Jag,' he said, as they came out of number 48 Ashley Road. His seven-year-old Cortina that overheated in summer and leaked in winter was standing by the kerb. 'Only that went with the job.'

'I know,' she said. 'Jade told me.'

It made him wonder what else Billy Grodzinski's daughter might have had to say about him. He didn't ask though and they drove in near-silence to the Peacock's Tail, a wine-bar he'd reconnoitred the night before. The decor was plush, the drinks overpriced and the background Muzak unobtrusive. It was, he hoped, the sort of place she'd be used to.

Jill asked for a white wine and soda, he had a bottle of lager and they sat at a marble-topped table that gave them a view of the other comings and goings at the bar. She had a subdued, almost weary air about her that made him wonder whether she regretted their arrangement. At least, though, he was becoming practised at carrying the conversation and asked her about her job at the school.

'Oh, it's all right,' she said. 'Well, the kids are all right. It's just the other members of staff who're a pain.'

'How long have you been there?'

'Just over a year.' As though wanting to get all the autobiographical stuff over with at one go, she added, 'I'd been married and then I got divorced and so I needed to get a job and that one just came along at the right time.'

He nodded, stuck for a response.

'Are you married, divorced or what?' she said.

'Oh no. Single. In fact I'm living with the old parents just now. Till I get something sorted.'

He was afraid it sounded juvenile, as though he'd somehow failed to get on with life. The truth was somewhat more complicated, involving three years in the Forces, a variety of motley bedsitters, eighteen months living with a barmaid in Stepney and two spells in prison. All of which he didn't want to get into at the moment.

They talked about books and he admitted his preference for autobiographies and American novels. He felt self-conscious, as though confessing to a secret vice. Besides, she was an expert and he was nervous about betraying himself through some foolish or naïve opinion.

She said she enjoyed going to the theatre, which left him high and dry since the only theatrical experience he could recall was the Raymond Revue Bar in Soho.

'However did you come to be a private investigator?' she asked.

64

Grateful for a safe subject, he told her about Clifford's death and how he'd been co-opted by Yvonne to serve as her partner.

'And I mean the really amazing thing was finding out they'd been having this wild affair for years. If you could see Yvonne . . . well, she's just not the type for wild affairs, not in a million years.'

But she didn't seem to share his amusement.

'And what is the type?'

'What?'

'You said she's not the type. Why not?'

'Well, because she, er . . . not much to look at,' he ended lamely.

'Oh, I see. And you think only beautiful people should have affairs?'

He hesitated, knowing they'd got locked into a confrontation without quite knowing how.

'I suppose not,' he said flatly. 'I've never thought much about it.'

'Obviously not.'

Resenting being put down, he let the conversation lapse. He'd been keyed up for their meeting, imagining he'd have to be on his toes to keep this classy bird entertained, but hadn't expected this strange, brooding hostility.

'Oh look, I'm sorry,' she said suddenly. 'I'm just not in a very good mood. It's nothing to do with you.'

'So what's it to do with?'

She shook her head. 'Oh, things generally. Look, let me buy you a drink. What do you want?'

He protested that he'd do the buying but she'd have none of it so he gave way, fearing she'd think him old-fashioned. After all, she probably earned more than he did.

'And so what're you working on at the moment?' she asked, returning from the bar with another bottle of

65

lager but nothing for herself.

'Oh, this and that. And one very dodgy number that we'd probably be better off without.'

'Why's that?'

He answered carefully, wanting to keep her entertained without giving too much away.

'Oh, it's somebody that's come to us on account of he thinks he's being blackmailed. So yours truly's supposed to find out the blackmailer.'

'Why doesn't he go to the police?'

'He can't. See, if he does . . .'

'Oh, of course!' she said, anticipating him. 'Because of whatever it is he's being blackmailed about?'

'Exactly.'

'So might that not be dangerous? I mean for you?'

'It's a bit more dangerous than chauffeuring little girls to school. But then it's a sort of friend of mine who's asked me to do it so . . .' His gesture suggested he hadn't had much choice.

'And are you getting anywhere?'

'Not really, no.'

'What, nowhere at all?'

'More or less.'

'But what'll happen then? Will this friend of yours pay up or what?'

Harry hesitated. He'd wondered that himself.

'Oh, shouldn't I be asking?' she said, mistaking his hesitation for professional discretion. 'Just tell me to shut up if you like.'

'No, it's not that,' he reassured her. 'Just that I don't know what he'll do.'

'Well, I hope you can help him. It'd be terrible if you couldn't.'

'I'll let you know what happens,' promised Harry. At least she was helping to strengthen his flagging commitment to the case. He'd like one day to be able to tell her he'd solved it.

It was only a short time later that she said, 'Would you mind if we went soon? Only I'm rather tired. It's just been one of those days.'

'First the kids, then me,' he joked, but there was a touch of sourness that didn't escape her.

'Don't be like that. I'm just tired, that's all.'

'Sorry,' he said stiffly, and they came out to the car with a coolness between them.

Where he'd gone wrong he couldn't say for sure. Only that the evening that should have brought them together and left them at ease in one another's company had misfired, leaving a space between them just about as wide as when they'd started.

'Would you like to come in for coffee?' she said when he dropped her off outside her flat.

It was such a forlorn offer, desperate for a refusal, that he had to smile.

'Would you be dead upset if I said no thanks?' he said, feeling free to tease a little now he'd nothing to lose.

'I know I've been a drag,' she sighed.

'No,' he felt obliged to protest. 'I've enjoyed it. I mean thanks for a . . . you know, a great evening.'

It was so transparently untrue that they both laughed and for a moment were brought together after all.

'You're a liar,' she said.

He didn't bother to deny it. 'Can I give you a ring sometime?'

'Yes,' she said. 'Please.'

'Well, er, cheers then.'

'Good-night,' she said and turned and hurried into the house.

Well, it'd been different, he thought, driving away. Not necessarily better than taking out one of the scrubbers from the local boozer but definitely different. Jill Hanscombe hadn't come tarted up and wearing her best diamanté ear-rings; she'd come in sweater and jeans

67

with ears well out of sight. She'd made no attempt to display a mood of gaiety or to drink herself into one but had remained casual and morose. And had then gone off to bed early and by herself.

Leaving the night still young and Harry driving back across central London and being reminded by a sign at the Marble Arch roundabout that he was passing close by Camden Town. And Camden Town, he was sure, was part of the address of Neil Patterson. He was struck by the thought that it would save him a journey and get another of his interviews over with if he were to visit him now.

He pulled up at the side of the road and took out the piece of paper Yvonne had given him: 2A Fizackerly Road, N4, was the address. Ten minutes later, and after consulting a map in the entrance to Camden Town tube, he'd found it.

Which was when his problems started since number 2A didn't seem to exist. There was a number 2 certainly but that, according to the brass plaque on the gatepost, was a vet's residence. Then came number 4, with no sign of 2A. Had the infallible Yvonne come unstuck for once?

Deciding he might as well make sure, Harry approached the front door of number 2. His knock was answered by a tall, young man who interrupted Harry's explanation at the first mention of '2A'.

'It's down the lane,' he explained patiently. 'Everybody misses it. You go down the lane and there's a house by itself at the end.'

Harry thanked him, then set off to investigate the direction he'd indicated. And, to his surprise, found he had indeed overlooked a narrow track that cut between numbers 2 and 4.

He peered down into what appeared to be pitch darkness. It was too risky to take the car: impossible to tell whether he'd ever be able to turn and get out again. But the torch he kept in the glove-compartment might be useful.

Using its pale beam to show him the rutted track at his feet, he advanced cautiously for thirty yards or so before coming to a gate. A sign on it said 'Private'. There was a bell below it and another sign – 'Ring for attention.'

Harry raised his finger to it, then stopped. 2A Fizackerly Road he'd taken to be one of a row, with street lights and passing traffic that would have allowed him quietly to introduce himself and explain his business without exciting alarm. This hideaway, with no visible lights at all, was the last thing he'd expected or wanted. He'd come back in daylight he thought: at least then he could see what he was letting himself in for.

Till suddenly he saw his shadow grow before him on the gate. He turned and was hit by a glaring light that made him squint and thrust a hand before his eyes. It was a car, coming towards him along the track, though he was too blinded to see it even when it came to within five yards of him and stopped.

He dropped his arms to his sides as if in surrender and stood waiting. There was the sound of car doors opening and two shadowy figures appeared, one on either side of the beams of light in which he was held.

We decide we're going for it on the last Thursday in October. Which is just time enough to get things sorted but not too much time so word gets round. Strange thing is how well we all work together. I mean there's usually one in any bunch that gets on everybody's wick or some stupid rivalry develops that threatens to cock up the whole shooting-match but this time – nothing. I don't mean we're all bosom pals, just that the job comes first. And then there's a feeling – hard to describe, but a definite feeling from early on – that if everybody keeps his bottle we really can make this one work and walk off with half-a-million. Also I'm not the only one that fancies this'll be his last. We're all of us getting past the tearaway stage and me, Les, Tommy and Frank are married men so we're looking to cut down on the risks and keep it water-tight. Now we've got the passes we spend a few days checking out the building. Going in in ones and twos like we're doing a job or something, then going up to the fourth floor and walking about, seeing where everything is and how long it takes to get from one place to another. There's a store-room that's near to the service-lift where we reckon we can bung the security guards and I go up one day with Ronnie and stand covering him while he checks out the lock so we can get ourselves a key for it. Something else we need a key for is the lift, one that'll over-ride all the buttons so that once we're in it with the money we can make sure it'll be bottom floor next stop and there won't be some berk stopping us on the second. So Ronnie goes in, all dressed up like a workman with a bag of tools, and he says to one of the security men, 'Scuse me mate, do you have a key to immobilise this lift while I check out the alarm system? For you, anything, says the security man, and hands it over. Ronnie says Much obliged, and goes off and makes an impression of the key and then brings it back. There you go, he says to the security man, you shouldn't have any more trouble with that. In a way it's the best part of any job is the planning. Makes you feel you're part of something a bit special, a bit secret. Course the wife notices there's something up 'cause I'm getting tenser as it gets nearer. If you get nicked again, she says, you can kiss goodbye to both me and the kids for good. Course I deny everything. 'Cause that's what we all swore we'd do — not a word to anybody outside the eight of us, not even to the missus. Especially not to the missus. That way we make sure our security's a damn sight better than anything Fleet have got.

VI

'I'm looking for a Mr Patterson,' said Harry, fumbling in his pocket for one of the Agency's printed cards.

'You've found him,' said a voice. 'So what d'you want?'

'I'd rather not explain out here,' said Harry, feeling at a ludicrous and dangerous disadvantage, the headlights still blinding him and his questioner no more than a dark outline beyond.

'Bring the car,' said the voice, apparently addressing the other man.

The invisible speaker then stepped forward, materialising as a burly, short-necked man, wearing a mohair suit that strained across the shoulders as he pushed open the gate. 'Come on,' he said abruptly and went towards the house, leaving Harry to follow. The house was revealed as not unlike its owner, squat and solid-looking. It had perhaps once been a barn or farmhouse before being engulfed by the city.

The car came crawling behind them as though shepherding Harry lest he should turn and run. Then the door of the house was opened, lights were switched on and Harry was able to look back and see a Mercedes with a tall, young man in a leather jacket and with close-cropped hair getting out of the driver's seat.

Obviously Neil Patterson was the older of the two; eight years ago the other would have more likely been in school than in a gang of villains.

Harry stepped into the stone-flagged hallway where

Neil Patterson had turned to wait for him. 'In there,' he was told, with a nod of the head that sent him into a large room that was a hybrid of elegant drawing-room and warehouse. It was crowded with furniture, paintings, statues and all manner of odds and ends that Harry took to be antique but that might have been manufactured the day before yesterday for all he knew about it. Evidently the house was business-premises as well as home.

He was followed in by the young man who eyed him up and down in a distinctly unfriendly fashion but said nothing. Then Neil Patterson came in and perched on the edge of a fancy-looking sofa.

Harry held out his card. Patterson nodded to the young man, who came forward, snatched it from Harry's grasp and held it out for Patterson to read.

Harry wondered whether he was employee or boyfriend, or possibly both. Two queers in the mock-antique business. It wouldn't be the first time.

Patterson gave a disdainful grunt: he wasn't impressed by the card.

'Bad time to call I suppose,' said Harry apologetically. 'Only I happened to be passing on other business.'

'So what's all this about?'

'I'm making enquiries on behalf of a client.'

'So?'

'So can we have a word in private?'

'No.'

Harry made a gesture that said OK, it was up to him.

'You don't have to worry about Andy,' said Patterson. 'My confidential secretary is Andy.'

The young man giggled.

A couple of queers, thought Harry. Not the best set-up he might have hoped for. He'd come up against queers before and knew the powerful freemasonry that united them against the rest of the world and made him

73

an enemy before he'd opened his mouth.

Still, he'd no choice but to say what he'd come to say. 'It's about a Mr Les Pinfield. I believe you once worked with him?'

'Oh yes? And what makes you believe that?'

'It's what I've been told.'

'Well, I think whoever told you is lying, don't you?'

'When I say worked with him,' said Harry, knowing he was withdrawing the pin from the grenade, 'I mean you were around when he was one of a gang that did Fleet Television for half-a-million quid. 'Bout eight years ago.'

'I hope you don't mean that,' said Patterson quietly.

Andy chuckled in appreciation.

'Look, I'm not interested in the robbery,' said Harry, though his hope of getting anywhere was now changing fast into a hope that he could get out in one piece. 'I've just got a job to do and that's to find out what happened to Les Pinfield before he died. I'm not working for the law and I'm not interested in whatever happened eight years ago, only as it affects Les.'

'You listening to this?' said Patterson to his companion.

Andy spoke for the first time, betraying a Scottish brogue. 'I'm listening but I can't believe it.'

That's all he needed, thought Harry resignedly. Not only queer – Scotch as well. A guaranteed nutter.

'You know that Les Pinfield was killed,' he said. 'You might have read about it in the papers.'

'And you've come to arrest us, have you?' said Patterson.

'No.'

'I'm relieved to hear it.'

With nowhere else to go, Harry struggled ever onwards. 'Before he was killed, there was somebody trying to blackmail him. Somebody sent him a letter saying that unless he paid up they'd blow the gaff on the 1977 job you all pulled. And Mrs Pinfield has asked me to find out whether anybody else might have been getting similar letters.'

It had to be a crazy way of making a living, this going round insulting professional villains on somebody else's behalf. Even Kamikaze pilots were given aeroplanes.

'So let's get this clear,' said Patterson. 'You're not only telling me I'm a thief. You're telling me there's blackmail letters that're down to me. And there's a murder that's down to me as well.'

'Not really,' said Harry quietly, knowing protest was useless.

'So what are you saying?' insisted Patterson. 'I mean, come on, Mr . . .' He looked again at the card which Andy had put down on a convenient escritoire. '. . . Mr Harry Sommers of the Sod-All Private Investigation Agency, what are you saying?'

'Mrs Pinfield asked me to enquire whether you'd also received any blackmail letters,' said Harry patiently.

'Andy,' said Patterson, 'do you know anything about this? Is it you that's sending these letters?'

'Not that I'm aware of, Neil.'

'No, well it couldn't be, could it? I mean you can't write, can you?'

And they both laughed.

'Sorry, chief,' said Patterson, turning back to Harry, 'we don't seem able to help.'

It occurred to Harry that attack might, after all, be the best form of self-defence.

'It's me that's trying to help you,' he said sharply. The two men looked at him. 'There's somebody onto you lot. And, whoever it is, he's going to screw as much as he can out of every one of you unless somebody can catch up with him first. Which is what I'm trying to do.'

There was a moment's silence when he thought he might have been winning, then Patterson said, 'Get rid of him.'

'Be a pleasure,' said Andy, and moved forward towards Harry who held up both hands in a gesture of surrender.

'No need for the strong-arm stuff. You want me to go – I'm going.'

'Too right you are,' said Andy, lunging at him.

Harry side-stepped and threw a short right hook into Andy's stomach. His leather jacket softened the blow but it was enough to pull him up with a grunt of dismay.

I shouldn't have done that, thought Harry. They're not going to like it.

'You stupid bastard,' said Patterson, crossing the room. He pulled a highly-polished stick down from a rack, unscrewed the top and revealed it to be a sword-stick with a wicked length of pointed steel.

Harry looked about him and grabbed the nearest thing, which was a marble statue of a naked woman. Held by the head, it made a passable club. Andy meanwhile was recovering his breath and muttering in unintelligible Glaswegian dialect.

Patterson waved the sword-stick. 'Come on, then! Come on if you fancy your chances!'

Harry grabbed a second statue that was sister to the first so that he had a female-shaped club in each hand. 'Now think about it,' he said, surprised at the steadiness of his voice since everything else, his heart, his whole body, was going ten to the dozen. 'Think about it.'

'What is there to think about?' said Patterson.

'The damage,' said Harry, inspired. 'The damage to all this expensive stuff. 'Cause I'm going out of here. And either I go out quietly or I go out leaving this place looking like a bomb's hit it.'

There was a moment when he thought they hadn't bought it, then Patterson let the sword-stick fall and said, 'Go on. Get out.'

'Oh no,' said Andy. 'No, I want that bastard. Him and me have something to settle.'

'Not here, Andy,' said Patterson. 'And not now either.'

'Some other time, eh, Andy?' said Harry.

The young man lunged forward but was stopped by a 'No!' from Patterson and by an upraised marble goddess in Harry's fist.

'I'll kill you,' he said. 'And that's a promise.'

'I won't hold you to it,' said Harry and, still carrying his marble clubs, he stepped towards the door. Neither of the two men moved to stop him. He reached the door, opened it with his foot and was out into the hallway.

He heard a yell from Andy – 'Bastard!' – and Patterson saying soothingly, 'It's all right', before he let fall the statues, flung open the front door and ran to the gate.

It resisted his first attempts to open it so he hauled himself up and over the top. Dropping to the ground on the other side, he could see the lights of the road at the end of the lane and ran thankfully towards them.

Having had enough escapades for one night, he went to one of his regular haunts for a much-needed drink which led to another and then another and then to his arriving late and suffering from a hangover at the office the next morning.

'Oh, thank goodness you've got here,' said Yvonne. 'I was beginning to think something must have happened.'

'It nearly did.'

'That Mr Holliday phoned. He says he wants to see

you and it's urgent so I told him you'd probably be free around eleven o'clock this morning. Is that all right?'

Not really, thought Harry. He could go a long time without seeing Phil Holliday if he was going to bring more trouble of last night's sort.

'I suppose it'll have to be,' he grunted.

'Oh, and while we're on the subject – I'm not getting very far with these other three names you want me to trace.'

'Good.'

She looked at him. 'Do you mean that?'

He couldn't have truthfully said yes or no so just shrugged and left her to make up her own mind.

'Only, if we do, we can always tell the client that we've failed to trace them and leave it at that.'

It was an attractive idea but he felt obliged to resist it. Whether it was the desperation of Phil Holliday or the earnest faith of Jill Hanscombe or just his own bloody-mindedness, he couldn't bring himself to throw in the towel. Anyway, not yet.

'No, we'd better keep trying.'

'Well, I've been round the usual credit agencies and they've come up with nothing.'

'So what's left? What about that DHSS computer you were telling me about?'

'Clifford used it only in dire emergencies,' she said. Which meant no, it wasn't a good idea. 'And we do have to pay our contact enough to make the risk worth his while.'

'Well, what else, then?'

'I really don't know. It's very difficult when it's just the names alone with nothing else to go on. Perhaps Mr Holliday could give you some more information?'

'I doubt it. Look, leave it for now. I've still got one more address to chase up. Then we'll have a think about what to do.'

'It's difficult for me to advise,' said Yvonne, 'since, of

course, I don't know anything about the case.'

'It must be,' he said, and left it at that.

With Phil Holliday due at eleven, he decided to stay in the office and do some paperwork – not his favourite part of the job – in fact, only marginally preferable to being attacked by queers with sword-sticks.

The odd thing was that, for all the hostility and downright violence with which Neil Patterson and side-kick had greeted him, he couldn't help feeling they were as innocent as new-born lambs when it came to the vexed question of who'd been sending blackmail letters and bumping off Les Pinfield. They just hadn't been interested, not even in persuading Harry they weren't involved. If Patterson had remembered Les Pinfield, it'd been as part of a murky past with which he now didn't care to be associated, thanks all the same. He also seemed to be doing quite nicely for himself, what with the house and the Merc and the rooms chock-a-block with antiques. There was the Glaswegian boy-friend to be paid for but, all the same, Harry couldn't see Patterson as a man desperate for ten thousand quid. Anyway, not desperate enough to kill Les Pinfield when he failed to cough up.

The paperwork quickly lost its appeal and he decided to have a quick glance at the newspaper before Phil Holliday was due to arrive. For the first time in his life he found himself stopping at the column of small-ads headed 'Theatres'. There seemed to be quite a lot of them: choosing wouldn't be easy.

'Have you ever been to the National?' he called to Yvonne.

'What, the horse-race?'

'No. Theatre.'

She shook her head. 'I wouldn't want to neither.'

Phil Holliday had come for a progress report and was dismayed to be told there hadn't been any.

79

'Oh, come on, Harry boy, you promised!'

'I promised nothing. I thought I made that clear if nothing else.'

'Well all right then, but I'm paying, aren't I? I mean you're going to be presenting me with a hefty bill at the end of all this and expecting me to pay it.'

Harry sighed, knowing he'd played it badly. He remembered Clifford's dictum: 'Never tell a client there's been no progress. Make it sound positive. Tell him you've made lots of progress but it's all been in eliminating false leads.'

'What I mean is – so far it's been more a matter of sorting out who hasn't sent the letters than who has.'

'So who have you seen?'

'Well, I saw Mrs Pinfield. . . .'

'I know. She told me,' said Phil impatiently. 'I mean the others. Who have you seen out of them?'

'I've seen Ronnie Franks. And I've seen Neil Patterson.'

'Is that all?'

'Give us a chance for Christ's sake!' expostulated Harry. 'This isn't bleeding Interpol you know. And it's not Sherlock Holmes either. It's just me going round sticking my neck out on your behalf.'

'OK, mate. OK,' said Phil, taken aback. 'I wasn't meaning to cast aspersions. I'm sure you're doing your best.'

But Harry hadn't finished. 'I nearly got into some very serious bother last night on your account. I tell you, I can do without this case. In fact, I can probably live a lot longer without it.'

Now Phil was alarmed. 'Hey, Harry boy, you're not going to let me down? I mean you're not, are you?'

Harry let him sweat a moment, then silently shook his head.

'Course you're not,' said Phil, relieved.

God alone knew, thought Harry, what he'd done to deserve Phil's trust. Not only had he so far discovered precisely nothing, but he couldn't see himself ever doing any better.

'So how did you find old Ronnie and Neil, then?' asked Phil.

'Ronnie Franks is running a second-hand car business. He got a bit nervy when I told him about the letters but I'll swear it was the first he'd heard of 'em.'

Phil nodded. 'I wouldn't have figured Ronnie for it. He was always all right was Ronnie. What about Neil, then?'

'You might have warned me he doesn't like being asked questions.'

'Turned nasty, did he?'

'He did. Him and his boy-friend both.'

'Now there you do surprise me. Turning nasty, yes, but turning pooftah, that I wouldn't have expected.'

'Well, that's how I read it. Not that I minded. Till it started looking like they wanted to share me between 'em.'

'So what do you reckon? I mean do you reckon he knew anything about the letters or what happened to Les?'

'No.'

Phil looked disappointed. 'You're sure? I mean if, like you say, he tried to put the frighteners on you . . .'

'He did that all right. But I'd still say – so far as I could judge – he didn't know the first thing about any letters. And, going by the set-up he has there, I wouldn't have said he needed the money either.'

'There's nobody got that much they can't use a bit more,' said Phil, then added quickly, 'But, all right, I'm not arguing. Only what am I supposed to do? I mean you can see where it leaves me, can't you, Harry boy? I'm still up to my neck right in it!'

81

'Yeah well, I'm sorry about that.'

'You're sorry. What d'you think I am?'

Scared to death, thought Harry. He only wished he could be more reassuring, hold out hope of a way out.

'I'm going to see Tommy Coyle next,' he said. 'We've got his address but we're still in the dark about the others. Can you think of anything that might help us find 'em?'

Phil shook his head. 'It's been a long time. And, like I say, the idea was that once the job was over it was everybody for himself. There was nobody wanting reunions or anything of that sort.'

'Well, we'll keep trying,' promised Harry. Then had an idea. 'I'll tell you what might help though. Can you have a word with this Tommy Coyle character? Get him to talk to me?'

'Well, how d'you mean?'

'Just tell him I'm not the law. Tell him Les Pinfield's widow has asked me to make some enquiries and it's all right for him to talk. Tell him what you like, only it'd be nice to talk to somebody who's on my side for a change.'

'Well OK, I'll do what I can,' said Phil, though clearly not keen. 'You've got his phone-number, have you?'

Harry gave him the number Yvonne had come up with and suggested Phil should try and arrange for himself and Tommy Coyle to meet tomorrow.

'And what do I do in the meantime?' said Phil. 'Do I put this sticker in the window like the letter said or do I not?'

'I don't see why not,' said Harry.

It would gain some time if nothing else. It would certainly gain some for Phil Holliday whose life might be in danger if he were to give the impression of not playing along.

'I've already gone and bought one,' he said, and

produced a West Ham badge from his pocket. It was the kind intended for car windows. 'I'll stick it up as soon as I get back.'

'You do that,' said Harry. 'Then all you'll have to worry about will be Chelsea supporters.'

Later, when Phil had gone, he tossed a coin to decide for him whether he should attempt to arrange another evening out with Jill Hanscombe. After all, there didn't seem to be any good reason one way or the other. Their first date had been fairly depressing but had ended on a moment of sudden warmth that might be the starting-point for their second. The coin came down tails, which meant that he wouldn't bother.

So he waited five minutes and tried again. This time it came down heads so he rang the National Theatre and asked about tickets. The reply told him that there were some but made the obstacles to getting them sound formidable.

The lady herself he tried later in the day when he'd calculated she'd had time to get home from school.

The phone was picked up after its second ring.

'Hello?' said Harry tentatively, hearing nothing from the other end.

'Yes?'

It was her all right, though sounding defensive and unwelcoming.

'It's me. Harry.'

'Oh hello. Yes.'

She did at least remember him, then.

'How are you?'

'Fine, yes.'

She obviously wasn't in a mood to be chatty – was she ever? – so he decided he might as well get to the point and asked her bluntly would she like to go to the theatre with him? He read out the name of the play from the newspaper. It was one he'd never heard of, which was probably in its favour.

There was no answer.

'Hello? Jill?'

'Yes, sorry. I just thought you weren't interested in the theatre, that's all.'

It was difficult to deny. 'It's something I've been meaning to get round to,' he said. 'Only I need to go with somebody who can tell me what it's all about.'

'Oh God, don't say that. Now you've really put me off.'

Great, he thought. At first she's not sure, then one word from him and her mind's made up: she never wants to go near the theatre again.

'Oh well . . .' Forget it, he was about to say, but before he could she asked: 'When were you thinking of going?'

'Oh . . . tomorrow? Any time. Or not at all if you don't want to.'

'No. No, I'd like to.'

'You would?' He tried to keep the surprise out of his voice.

'It's a play I haven't seen and it's had a good review in the *Guardian*.'

'Has it? And what about the *Sun*? What do they think?'

'Pardon?'

'Forget it. A joke. I'll pick you up, shall I?'

They agreed on a time and she'd put the phone down before he could say any more.

It started to ring again later that evening just as Harry was about to leave the office. Yvonne had already gone, leaving him alone.

It'll be her, he thought. Miss High-and-Mighty Jill Hanscombe. She's had second thoughts and is ringing to cancel. Well, that's it. That is well and truly it. Even a classy bird that reads the sodding *Guardian* can take only a certain number of liberties before she gets an earful.

He snatched up the phone. 'Yes?'

There was a silence. It's her all right, he thought. A tease even when it came to talking on the bleeding phone. Well, he'd had it up to here and now he was going to enjoy letting her know it.

But, when it finally did come, the voice on the other end wasn't hers at all.

'Is it you that's been asking questions about Les Pinfield?'

When Harry had the chance to think about it afterwards, he would be confident only that the voice was male and sounded muffled, as though through a handkerchief.

'Is it what?' said Harry, gathering his scattered wits.

'Only you're taking a very big risk. You do know that, don't you?'

'Who's speaking?'

'Never mind. Just drop it, OK? Just stay well clear if you value your health.'

And a click as the receiver was replaced.

The week before we're due to pull it off we all get ourselves into the building to watch the money being delivered. A sort of dry-run. I'm in the foyer with Tommy Coyle who's going to be there on the day using a sort of bleeper device – like you see doctors wearing – to cue us on the fourth floor as to what's going on downstairs. We watch the van arrive and it's one of these converted Transit jobs with armour-plating and wire-grilles over the windows. It stops as near as it can to the front entrance then four blokes in all the gear get out and unload six metal boxes onto a wooden trolley. They're looking round all the time like they're half-expecting to be jumped. Then they're across the pavement and into the foyer and it's Morning and All right and How're you to the Fleet security men who're holding the doors for 'em. Vince Jardine has been shitting himself wondering if they've changed the routine so that our plan won't work any more and he'll end up getting it in the neck since it's been his idea in the first place. But no, they do it just like he's said they would. Money into the lift and two of the guards in with it while the other two wander back to their mini-tank they've left parked on double yellows outside. Later on we all meet up back at the flat and Ronnie reports how the blokes from the cash office wait on the fourth floor, then the lift arrives and they trundle off down the corridor with the money – the guards going with 'em as far as the cash office so's they can have their trolley back. So Vince is well pleased 'cause it seems like everything he's told us is one hundred-per-cent accurate. There is just one problem though and it's Maurice that tells us about it. He's going to be driving one of the motors and he's been checking things out from the loading-bay end, making sure everything's clear for the getaway. Well, he tells us we'd never get that trolley out in a month of Sundays on account of there's all sorts of junk cluttering up the area that's between the lift and the doors where we want to come out. So there's some debate about this and it's agreed somebody'll have to be stationed down there to make sure we have a clear run from the lift to the loading-bay. Which nobody wants to do *since it seems like a cop-out from the real business. In the end it's a choice between me and Neil Patterson and we cut a pack of cards and he draws a seven and as luck would have it I draw an eight. It's already been arranged that Frank's firm will see to nicking the motors. We talk about what we'll wear and decide on no stockings or masks since if things go to plan we'll be away before anybody knows what's happening and eight of us wandering around with Mickey Mouse faces'll be as good as announcing over the Tannoy that there's robbers in the building. And no clever make-up since we have to look like the photos on our passes. For weapons everybody provides his own. But no shooters and no knives. We don't want a killing, even by accident, 'cause that way they'll come after us for ever whereas half-a-million quid they'll have forgotten about inside of three weeks.*

VII

Phil Holliday contacted Harry next morning to say he'd
been in touch with Tommy Coyle who didn't mind
talking to Harry and might even buy him a drink if he
cared to drop in at the Blind Beggar pub in Bethnal
Green that lunchtime.

Harry promised he would. Phil's speed in making the
arrangement showed just how scared he must be. After
all, Les Pinfield had been killed no more than a week
after receiving his letter. On that basis Phil was already
living on borrowed time.

As for the warning to lay off that Harry himself had
received, well, he could live with it for the time being.
At least it suggested he was getting somewhere: though
it was a surprise to realise it, he must be near enough to
his adversary to have provoked him into issuing his
threat.

He'd have to be careful, but then he always was. His
motley career of boxer, bouncer and minder had made
him familiar with physical danger. The only extra
element here – admittedly a disturbing one – was the
murder of Les Pinfield to remind him that this was a
warning deserving more than the customary pinch of
salt.

Still, meeting Tommy Coyle should be safe enough.
He shouldn't come to much harm in a public-house and
in broad daylight. Even if the pub had earned itself a
certain notoriety in the mid-sixties when Ronnie Kray
had entered the public bar with a gun in his hand and
shot George Cornell through the head. That had been a

time when London's gangland resembled the old Wild West; things had calmed down since then.

Harry's immediate problem was more prosaic: how could he find time to get hold of the tickets he needed for the evening? He mentioned the problem to Yvonne, hoping she'd take the hint.

'I see,' she said archly. 'And it's a young lady you're taking, is it?'

Harry nodded. 'If I can get the tickets.'

'Would you like me to try for you?'

He put on a small display of surprise and reluctance: 'Well, are you sure? I mean if you're not too busy . . .'

'I might not be able to trace addresses but I'm sure I can ring a theatre. You'd better tell me exactly what you want.'

He showed her the newspaper and underlined the name of the play.

'What's it about?' she asked.

'I haven't a clue.'

'My, you must be keen.'

Must I? he thought. And just what was he keen on – Jill Hanscombe in particular, or the thought of going out with a bird you could take to the theatre and know she wouldn't sit facing the wrong way? Perhaps tonight would answer that question for him.

Wanting to reciprocate Yvonne's show of interest in his love-life, he asked, 'And how's the Chinese boyfriend, then?'

'Oh, all right. Though I'm going off him a bit to tell you the truth.'

'A case of sweet and sour is it?'

She gave a little laugh, then said, 'More a case of him being only interested in one thing. And it's not cooking either.'

Harry nodded, deciding not to enquire further. If the Orient had its mysteries, they were as nothing beside those of Yvonne.

His visit to the Blind Beggar had to be fitted between an increasing number of other commitments as the Agency now seemed to be finding its feet again, meaning that Harry was beginning to be rushed off his. As well as the steady work of process-serving for Samuel, Jessop and King, who seemed to have overcome their initial doubts about the new management, other cases had started to turn up: a missing person to be traced, a husband who wanted his wife following, and a mistress who wanted somebody else's husband following. It was an eye-opener, this trickle of apparently normal people whose lives were in all kinds of confusion. Having spent most of his own life beyond the pale of respectability, Harry shared the prejudices of most villains, believing that everyone but for themselves led a boring and settled existence. Not true, he was now finding. You couldn't open a suburban cupboard door without a skeleton or two coming clattering out.

So it was something of a relief to be resting an elbow on the bar of the Blind Beggar and accepting the offer of a drink from Tommy Coyle. The place had a familiar, comfortable feel to it. A lot of the drinkers were familiar as well. There was a fair smattering of small-time villains and a few older hands who were more or less past it but liked to be around those that weren't.

Tommy Coyle might have come into this category. He was an untidily dressed man in his mid-forties with a day's growth of beard that added to his rather defeated and discontented air. But he'd greeted Harry amiably enough and seemed eager to talk, a pleasant change from the Neil Pattersons of this world.

They sat at a table. Tommy took out a tin of tobacco and began to roll himself a thin cigarette.

'Phil told you what I'm trying to do, did he?' asked Harry.

'He did. It was good to talk to him again as well. You don't half get out of touch with people in this game. If they're doing well they go and live on the Costa Brava. And if they're not they end up in the nick. Either way they're not around much.'

'I suppose not.'

'Haven't seen old Phil for donkey's years.'

'He did tell you that all this is confidential, did he? I mean whatever you tell me – it'll go no further.'

Tommy nodded. 'Fair sang your praises he did. Said I could tell you things I wouldn't tell my own brief.'

'Good of him.'

'He said it's about that wages job we pulled about, oh, be seven or eight years ago.'

'It is. I just want you to tell me as much as you can remember about it.'

'Oh well, I remember it all right. Best team I ever worked with that was. Could do with something like that again, I can tell you.'

'You remember Les Pinfield, worked on it with you?'

'Les, oh yes. I remember 'em all. You work on something like that – something as good as that – and you don't forget in a hurry. Mind you, Phil tells me Les has come to a sticky end, is that right?' Harry nodded. 'I didn't know. I'm so out of touch, you see.'

'He was stabbed. And the word is it was somebody trying to put the arm on him over this robbery. Pay up or else.'

Tommy shook his head in dismay. 'And he didn't pay up, then?'

'Well, not as far as we know.'

'That's diabolical.' He raised his glass. 'Well, here's to old Les, then. And let's hope that the bugger that did it gets all that's coming to him.'

'Let's hope so,' said Harry.

Tommy drained his glass and Harry went to the bar for more drinks. With nothing specific to go on, his best ploy was probably to sit back and listen while Tommy did the talking. Which he seemed willing enough to do.

91

Perhaps eight years was a long time to keep quiet about a job that'd gone so well and, like Phil Holliday, he'd be glad of the chance to talk freely at last.

'You haven't had anybody putting the arm on you, then?' asked Harry, coming back to the table.

'Me? No. Wouldn't do 'em a lot of good either unless it was dogs they was after.'

'Dogs?' said Harry, thinking he must have misheard.

'Dogs. Anybody comes to me for dogs they can have as many as they likes and welcome.'

'You, er, keep dogs, do you?'

'I keep well away from 'em. Well away. Filthy, noisy, bloody things. It's the wife that keeps 'em. That's where my money's gone is that. That's what I risked getting ten years inside for – so that now I can't step outside without getting dog-shit on me shoes.'

With nothing to say to that, Harry nodded sympathetically. Tommy began to roll another wafer-thin cigarette and then, his outburst over, explained in calmer tones: 'She's always been mad on dogs has the missus. So four years back, or more now, I dunno, she persuades me to take what money I have left and put it into starting a kennels. Biggest mistake I ever made.'

'I see.'

'Proper dog's life I have. All she cares about is them noisy bleeders. I'd have never gone on that Fleet job if I'd known what it was going to lead to.'

Harry seized the chance of directing him back to the matter in hand. 'How did it get off the ground? Who was it set the job up?'

'Well, it was a North London firm really. And they had some sort of connection with Les and they asked him if he'd got two or three reliable mates he could bring in on it. On account of it was too big for just the four of them.'

'And they were Frank Metcalf, Maurice Scanlon, Vince Jardine and Neil Patterson . . .?'

'That's it. And then there was me, Les, Phil and, er . . .'

'Ronnie Franks.'

'That's him. How is he, old Ronnie, have you seen him?'

'He's selling second-hand motors.'

'Is he, now? It's what I should have done is that. 'Stead of bleeding dogs. See, that was the thing about this job – there was a lot fancied making it the one last big one and then getting out. That was why nobody went round shouting about it I suppose.'

'So what happened after you'd all got together, then?' prompted Harry.

Tommy completed his roll-up and launched himself into an account of the robbery that more or less followed the same course as the one Harry had already heard from Phil Holliday. The only real difference was that Tommy played up his own role as coordinator, the man positioned in the foyer directing operations. Harry fancied it was because he'd been the one with the least bottle for the aggro but he didn't bother to suggest it. Just got up at regular intervals and went to the bar to refill Tommy's glass.

His only reason for wanting to hear it all related again was a faint hope of finding some significant discrepancy between the two accounts or of picking up some hint of an antagonism or rivalry that over eight years might have grown into blackmail and murder. But nothing of the sort emerged and Tommy's rambling story came to its end, the same end that Phil had recounted with the dividing of the spoils and the going of their separate ways.

'Best thing I ever worked on,' mused Tommy nostalgically. 'I tell you, one of them every six months and she could keep the dogs. I'd be off living on the Costa Brava. Don't have much time for dogs there, do they?'

Looking at his watch and seeing it was time he was moving, Harry tried a final question.

'It can't have been all that perfect surely. Wasn't there ever anything looked like going wrong?'

'Nothing, no. Well, 'cept we could have done without the way everything was nearly cocked up at the end.'

Harry waited, then said quietly, 'And what was that, then?'

But Tommy, sensing a new interest in his listener, had become cautious. 'Oh, nothing, just . . . Did Phil not mention?' Harry shook his head. 'Oh well, it wasn't anything special. Just people getting nervy before the off, that was all.'

Harry had the distinct feeling that that wasn't all and that there was something more but Tommy had shut up shop and even the offer of another drink failed to start him talking again.

'I'll tell you what you could do though,' he said.

'What's that?'

'I wouldn't mind a lift. You going anywhere near the Mile End Road?'

Strictly speaking, Harry was going in the opposite direction but he didn't mind the detour if there was a chance he might learn more about this last-minute cock-up. He tried to raise the subject again when they were in the car.

'No, it was nothing,' insisted Tommy. 'Just everybody getting nervy, that's all. You know what it's like with two firms working together. Then we had a meeting at Frank's flat to sort it all out and everybody went away happy.'

Phil Holliday's account had included reference to a meeting the night before the job. Perhaps that really had been it, then. Odd, though, the way Tommy had clammed up on that single question.

Remembering the problems Yvonne was having

tracing the remaining addresses, he asked, 'You don't know where I might find Frank Metcalf by any chance?'

'Frank? No. North London somewhere he was.'

'Maurice Scanlon?'

Tommy shook his head. 'North London again.'

'Vince Jardine?'

To his surprise this last name produced a result.

'Well, not now, no. But I can tell you where he was living then. 'Cause even though he like hung about in North London it turned out he was from the East End and him and me was nearly neighbours.'

'Do you remember the address?'

'I can tell you the block of flats he was in. But not the number.'

Harry pulled a note-pad from his pocket and asked him to write down the address as far as he remembered it. Even an eight-year-old lead was too good to pass up. Clifford had often waxed lyrical on the thousand and one ways of tracing someone given even an old address. There were the neighbours, the pub at the end of the road, the newsagent, the milkman. If you struck really lucky there might even be a local firm that'd done the removal and could give you the new address.

They came to Mile End Road and Tommy directed him where to turn. 'Over there,' he said as they came to the end of a street and Harry saw what had once been a garage with a sign 'Mile End Kennels' hanging over the forecourt.

'Only chance I have,' said Tommy, 'is that the neighbours keep threatening to get up a petition because of the noise.' He got out of the car. 'Just watch me give 'em a bit of encouragement.'

Harry, fascinated, stayed where he was and watched as Tommy picked up a fist-size stone from the ground, checked he was unobserved, then flung it over the sign. The stone clanged and clattered its way across the corrugated roofing that was behind. A chorus of

95

barking and yelping started up from within.

Tommy, grinning broadly, turned and gave Harry a thumbs-up sign. Harry laughed, gave a toot on his horn and drove off.

The National Theatre surprised him by looking more like a posh airport than a theatre. Signs assured him the auditoriums were tucked away somewhere but all he could see, as they stood sipping their drinks, were acres of carpet between walls of grey concrete.

Jill seemed in brighter mood than before and looked as classy as any of the other women around them in her leather boots and a black corduroy outfit. Harry felt staid in his collar and tie and three-piece.

She asked him about the blackmail case he was working on. Had he solved it yet?

Not sure whether she was teasing or in earnest, he smiled and said, 'Not yet, no. I've three more suspects to see, then . . . well, then I probably still won't have solved it.'

'But what are you looking for? What's going to be the vital clue?'

If only he knew.

'Oh, I dunno,' he said. 'What do you think I should be looking for?'

She rose to the challenge. 'Well,' she said, 'as far as I can see, there are two basic approaches, aren't there?'

'And what're they?'

'Well, first of all there's the forensic, right? Where it's all a matter of fingerprints and handwriting and you do a microscopic analysis of the dust particles that're inside the envelope and the dust particles from the homes of the various suspects. But I don't suppose you do that?'

'I don't suppose I do, no.'

'Well then, method number two is more your sort of intuitive approach.'

'And what's that?'

'Oh, you know, questioning the suspects, getting to know them, tying them in knots with penetrating questions. All that. And then your years of experience come into play to help you make your final judgement.'

'No,' he said, 'I don't do that either.'

'Well then, there's only one way left,' she said. 'Put the names in a hat and draw one out.'

He laughed. 'It might come to that. But, don't forget, I do have another way out as well.'

'What?'

'I can always give up. Just pack it in. I'm not the law. I don't have to get results. I can say sorry but – finito.'

'Oh, but you wouldn't,' she protested.

'I might have to.'

'But you'll try everything you can first?'

'If you insist.'

'I do. I feel sorry for this whoever-he-is that's being blackmailed.'

'Perhaps if you knew him you wouldn't feel as sorry. He's not exactly one of your good citizen types.'

She looked him in the eye. 'And you think I go for good citizen types, do you?'

He was saved from having to answer by an announcement that their play would be starting in three minutes. Though it seemed a shame that, just as they were becoming at ease with one another, they should be hustled away to see some play in which he hadn't the slightest interest. He almost suggested skipping it and going for a curry but suspected he'd come too far to duck out now.

At least the seats were comfortable. Too comfortable in fact. He knew after ten minutes that it was going to be a battle to stay awake. No disrespect to the play. The actors all seemed very good and knew their lines, of which there were a hell of a lot. It was just that at that time of the day he often had a quick doze in preparation for an evening's boozing ahead.

One thing that did help jolt him into wakefulness was when one of the actors started effing and blinding. Not just swear-words but your real four-letter jobs. He glanced sideways in alarm, fearing he'd see Jill jumping out of her seat. But no. She was showing no reaction at all; nor, so far as he could see, was anyone else.

He thought of a party he'd once attended to celebrate the release of Joey Bruchianni from prison where he'd served seven years for extortion and grievous bodily harm. The place was full of pimps and racketeers, one of whom had been sufficiently indiscreet to use the word 'bollocks' in the hearing of Mrs Joey Bruchianni (who'd traded in Greek Street under the name of 'Cindy' before catching her employer's eye). The offending guest had been grabbed by the hair by Joey, made to apologise to Mrs Bruchianni and then tossed out into the street since, whoever he was, he clearly didn't know how to behave himself in company.

Let's hope Joey never brings his missus to the National Theatre, thought Harry.

They came out for the interval. Harry fought his way through the pack at the bar and came away with a white wine and soda for Jill and a lager for himself.

'Well,' she said, 'and how're you liking it?'

'It's all right,' he said cautiously. 'How're you?'

She nodded. 'Yes. Very good.'

'Language is a bit ripe,' he ventured.

'Oh, do you think so?' She smiled. 'Don't tell me you've never heard the words before.'

'I've heard 'em all right. Even used 'em occasionally in the heat of the moment. Just didn't expect to hear 'em here, that's all.'

He was afraid he was sounding old-fashioned again.

The talk filling the air around them was like the high-pitched chatter of starlings; as if everybody had to say as much as they could before the interval would be up and the rule of silence reinforced.

As he feared, Harry dozed off soon after the start of the second act and was only awoken by a loud shout as the action of the play hotted up. He looked quickly at Jill but she seemed engrossed in the drama and, with luck, might not have noticed his having been asleep. Eventually the play ended to sustained applause and they came out into the foyer.

Jill rattled on, as starling-like as the rest, about the play which seemed to have pleased her. It was a relief since he'd chosen it at random and had no forewarning of its content.

'But did *you* like it?' she asked as they walked out to the car. 'Come on. Be honest.'

So he was. 'Not a lot, no.'

'You didn't?'

'Oh, I've enjoyed going,' he hurriedly reassured her. 'But that particular play – well no, I didn't think it was too marvellous.'

'Is that why you fell asleep?'

'I didn't think you'd noticed,' he said, abashed.

'Well, I did.'

They drove off, heading westwards.

'So do you fancy a drink or something to eat or what?' he asked, not knowing what might be the most suitable after a theatrical evening and, anyway, still not knowing her well enough to anticipate her preferences.

'Well, would you like to come back to the flat and have a drink there?'

It was an invitation as intriguing as it was unexpected and certainly not to be refused. He drove to Ashley Road and stopped before number 48. At that time of night the area was quiet with no-one about in the streets.

She led him up to flat 5, unlocked the door and went in before him, switching on the lights.

'Come on in, then!' she called. 'What are you waiting for?'

99

He entered and found himself in a room in which everything was remarkably simple. The walls were painted white; the carpet was beige and patternless; ornaments and pictures were at a minimum. Only books seemed to have licence to spread themselves: they overspilled their bookcases to form untidy piles on the floor and windowsills.

'Well,' she said, pulling a face. 'This is it. The trouble is I still feel it's sort of temporary so I can't seem to get round to doing anything about it.'

'It's nice,' he said, meaning it.

'Well, at least it's warm. I don't mind too much what it's like so long as it's warm. Now, I've got some wine and some beer. Which would you like?'

While she was sorting out the drinks, he took a look at her books. It was a random and varied collection. Harry, who was a reader but not a collector, was struck by the sheer number of books and their prominence in the scheme of things.

(His acquaintances were likewise bookless. The nearest to an exception being Billy Grodzinski who'd bought a comprehensive set of the *Encyclopaedia Britannica* for his daughter, Jade, and had taken Harry into the lounge to show him where it stood in its own mahogany bookcase next to the drinks cabinet.)

'You can borrow one if you like,' said Jill.

Harry muttered his thanks, but choice seemed impossible. Till she came to his side and picked one out.

'Didn't you say you liked American novels? This is fairly new. And I've finished it so there's no rush to get it back.'

He took it carefully from her, liking the idea of borrowing something of hers. It would be a tie of a sort and meant he'd have to come back if only to return it.

'Do I remember you saying you lived at home with your parents?' she asked.

'I am doing now,' he admitted. 'Only till I find

100

somewhere to move to.'

'And you're very choosy?'

'Not really. It's just that I can't face the hassle of looking.'

'What happened to your last place, then?'

'My last place was prison.'

She stared at him open-mouthed in surprise. His own surprise was almost as great. Why the hell did I say that? he thought. What am I trying to do, persuade her to throw me out?

'It was quite a while ago,' he muttered. 'I don't mean I was released last week or anything.'

'And what were you in for? If you don't mind my asking.'

He didn't. In fact, he welcomed the chance to make clear it hadn't been anything to do with raping women living alone.

'Assault, that sort of thing.' He shrugged. 'It sort of went with the job. Well, in my case it always seemed to.'

She frowned. 'It went with the job of being a private investigator?'

'Bouncer.'

'Oh, I see. And what was it like in prison?'

'Boring. Mind you, you got plenty of time for reading.'

She smiled. 'I'm sure you did.'

She wasn't going to throw him out then, ex-con or not. He began to relax again. And his revelation had certainly given them a topic for conversation. She wanted to know about the routine of the day, what were the worst things, what had he felt like on coming out.

'I was only in for six months,' he felt bound to protest. 'It wasn't like a life-sentence or anything.'

He didn't bother to mention it'd been his second visit to the Scrubs as a guest of Her Majesty. No point in pushing his luck too far.

It also wouldn't do to overstay his welcome. This was a working lady who had to get up in the morning. He refused a second drink and thanked her for going with him to the theatre.

'Even if you didn't enjoy it,' she teased.

'Even if I didn't.'

She opened the door and stood back to let him pass, then said, 'Oh, wait.' She went back into the room and returned with the book. 'Did you want it?'

'Oh yes, sure,' he said, taking it.

Doubts about the theatre might remain but not about her and about the fact that he wanted to see her again. Anything that might help that, even a book, was to be grabbed at.

It was as he drove away down Ashley Road, with the book on the seat beside him, that he noticed someone sitting alone in one of a line of parked cars. Then, slowing down to turn at the end, he looked in his mirror and saw that the car was pulling out and coming down the road after him.

In itself, of course, that meant nothing. Simply another late-night visitor to Ashley Road leaving at the same time. It began to mean something more when Harry checked his mirror again at the next junction and found the car still on his tail. He accelerated. The other car did the same, staying fifty yards or so behind him.

It was a blue Datsun. The driver was male and alone, but more than that it was impossible to tell.

Harry thought of the telephoned warning that he was to lay off the Les Pinfield case if he valued his health. But he hadn't laid off it. He'd gone that lunchtime to meet Tommy Coyle. So now here was his unseen enemy come to show that he'd been serious.

OK, thought Harry, let him try, let him have a go. He unclipped his safety-belt and let it slide off him. He thought of the torch in the glove-compartment but rejected it as a weapon. And there wasn't much else in the car if the other man were to come at him with a knife as Les Pinfield's fate suggested he might.

Aware that he might still be jumping to conclusions. Harry took the next turn left, and then left again, intending to go round the block to see if the other man would follow. And, sure enough, there he was, reappearing in the mirror after the first corner and then again after the second.

Harry took another left turn, drove along for thirty yards, then jammed everything on so that his car skewed to a halt. He opened the door and jumped out – just as the Datsun came following him round the corner.

There was a squealing of tyres as the driver, seeing Harry waiting, pulled his car in a vicious U-turn across the road, mounting the pavement and scraping the wall in the process. Another three inches and he'd have been stuck on the wall. As it was, there was a shower of sparks, then he was accelerating away and disappearing back round the corner.

Caught by surprise, Harry thought too late of getting the number. HBZ he thought as he bundled himself back into his own car. They, or something like them, were the first three letters but he'd no idea of the rest.

Knowing he'd no chance of turning as the Datsun had done, he drove to the other end of the road and turned left, hoping to catch sight of the other car retracing its path. But either he was too late or the other driver had anticipated him and had driven off in a different direction altogether. Harry cursed him, and cursed his own stupidity for not making sure he'd got the number earlier when he'd had the car well in his sights. He spent a fruitless ten minutes cruising around the area before deciding it was a waste of time and setting off for home.

There's a last meeting at Frank's flat in Islington the night before we're due to go. Everybody's edgy 'cause suddenly you're thinking of everything that can go wrong and what'll happen if it does. And there's a lot of mistrust coming out – between the two firms, each wondering whether they can count on the other. Still they've got the motors, nicked from out in Oxford or somewhere. One's a Volvo, which Les has a gripe about on account of he's once been on a job where a Volvo let 'em down badly but everybody else tells him to piss off so he shuts up about it, and the other's a Jag, which everybody likes the sound of. Even Les. There's one other vehicle we're using as well and that's a Volkswagen dormobile that's been picked up at auction. The idea is to use the Volvo and the Jag for the job, then head west to Holland Park, switch to the Volkswagen and head back north to Kentish Town where Neil Patterson has some sort of warehouse property. We do the share-out there and then split. There's a general agreement that we won't be meeting again. Not that anybody'll want to anyway 'cept perhaps that I'll still see Les occasionally since he's a mate from way back. And all of a sudden you can't wait for it to be over then it'll be every man for himself and sod the rest.

VIII

Before going any further with the case, Harry wanted to speak to Phil Holliday again. He rang him at the shop.

'You've found who it is?' asked Phil eagerly when Harry identified himself.

''Fraid not. Just wondered if you could help me, that's all.'

'How?'

'Well, what can you tell me about Vince Jardine?'

'Have you found him?'

'Well, not yet,' said Harry, sorry he wasn't able to offer any of the good news Phil was so desperate to hear. 'Only I've got a lead and, before I do catch up with him, I just want to know is he going to be a Neil Patterson-type nutter?'

'Well, no. He wasn't a bad sort, wasn't Vince.'

'You don't sound too sure.'

'Well come on, Harry boy, it's been a long time. People change, don't they?'

Not a lot, thought Harry. At least he'd never met anybody who had. But he had something else he wanted to ask.

'You remember you talked about the meetings you had when you were planning the job.'

'Yes?'

'You said they were at Frank Metcalf's flat in Islington. Where in Islington exactly?'

'You've got me there,' admitted Phil. 'I wouldn't know where to start. See, it was Les that knew the

105

address and it was always Les that drove us there.'

And Les certainly isn't going to be telling, thought Harry. Perhaps it was a question he could put to Vince Jardine if he caught up with him.

'I've put it in the window, Harry.'

'What's that, then?'

'The badge. The West Ham badge.'

'Oh yes. Let me know if it gets any reaction.'

'I'm just wondering if it's big enough. Whether I shouldn't have got a bigger one. Only, see, I don't want the missus to notice it and think I've gone barmy.'

'I'm sure it's big enough,' said Harry soothingly. 'Whoever's behind this is going to be keeping his eyes open.'

'Let's hope so.'

But Harry still had more to ask about the meetings. Even if the exact venue had become lost in the mists of time, the significance of that final meeting had begun to loom larger since his talk with Tommy Coyle.

'You remember you said there was a last meeting the night before the job. What was that in aid of?'

There was a pause, then: 'Well, just to, you know, iron out last-minute hitches. That sort of thing.'

'Tommy Coyle seemed to think it was for a lot more than that.'

'Why, what did he say about it?'

Did he sound worried or was it just Harry's imagination? Difficult to tell over the phone. His own fault for being lazy. He should have taken the trouble to go round to the shop and talk to him face to face.

'He seemed to think the whole thing was on the point of falling through. Then that last meeting was called and everybody got happy again.'

'Falling through?' said Phil, sounding more confident. 'That's coming it a bit strong is that. Like I say, there were one or two last-minute hitches, people

106

getting jumpy, that was all.'

Harry let it go. What did it matter anyway if there had been some problem that, for reasons of their own, both Phil and Tommy were keen to gloss over? It would still be an unlikely graduation from that to murder and blackmail eight years on.

'By the way,' he said, 'a blue Datsun. Does that remind you of anybody?'

'Nobody. Why?'

'Oh, nothing much. Just wondered, that's all.'

And he rang off.

It was something he'd been wondering about since last night's strange encounter. In particular he'd been wondering why his adversary should have set out to follow him so boldly and with little attempt at concealment but should then have turned and fled when Harry had stopped to face him. Perhaps he'd never intended anything more than a reminder to Harry of his warning that Harry should lay off the case, so that the prospect of actual confrontation had been unwelcome, something as yet to be avoided. Or perhaps Harry's tactics had wrong-footed him and he'd fled only so that, later, there'd be a confrontation for which the time and place would be of his own choosing.

Whatever the reason, Harry was clearly getting close enough to the blackmailer to be worrying him into showing his hand.

A more chilling thought was that the blackmailer was close enough to Harry to know who he was and where he'd be when he wanted to find him.

The address Tommy Coyle had scribbled down was for a block of flats in Whitechapel. Harry located it easily enough in the office *A to Z*, but then feared he was going to have to walk to get there. His car, susceptible to the drop in temperature as autumn got into its stride,

107

refused to start. It took a messy ten minutes cleaning plugs and leads before he could coax it into life. How long, he wondered, before he could talk to Yvonne about getting a new one on the firm?

Arriving in Whitechapel, he calculated there were perhaps fifty or sixty flats altogether, rising to eight storeys. It shouldn't be too difficult to discover if Vince Jardine were still a resident; though if he weren't, it might be a sight more difficult to find somebody who remembered him and knew where he'd gone.

Harry knocked on the first door he came to but got no reply and so moved on to the second. This was opened on a safety-chain so that he found himself talking to someone he could barely see. He explained his quest but got no more than a curt 'Never heard of him' before the door was closed again.

He was moving patiently on to door number three when he was overtaken by a postman delivering the second post of the day. Not one to look a gift-horse in the mouth, especially one that might save him a couple of hours' knocking on doors, Harry hurried after him.

''Scuse me.' The postman stopped. He was a young man with long sideburns, above which his cap was set at a rakish angle. 'Only I'm trying to find somebody. Name of Jardine. You don't happen to know 'em, do you?'

'Jardine?' The postman flicked through his handful of letters, then shook his head. 'Sorry, mate.' Then, as Harry's hopes fell, he added, 'Oh. Hang about', and reached into his bag for another bundle.

Harry waited while he looked through these.

'Yes, here we are. Number forty-three you want.'

'Great,' said Harry, beaming. It was the kind of break that made a private investigator's day. Made it a damn sight easier anyway.

Approaching number 43, he steeled himself for

whatever his reception might be. Judging from his experiences so far, Vince Jardine might well be happy enough to talk freely about the Great Fleet Television Robbery – relishing the memory of how everything had gone like clockwork – or he might be happier attacking Harry with a sword-stick. There was no way of telling but to knock on the door.

It was opened by a frail-looking, grey-haired woman who must have been in her seventies.

'Oh, sorry,' stammered Harry, thinking either he or the postman had made a mistake. 'I'm looking for a Mr Jardine.'

But no. The old woman nodded in recognition of the name: evidently there was no mistake.

'Would you wait a minute please,' she said, and disappeared.

Harry waited. He supposed she must be Vince Jardine's mother. At least her presence might lessen the likelihood of her son turning violent.

There was a shuffling sound as a man in his carpet slippers made his slow way to the door. He was, if anything, even older than the woman and wheezed from the effort of movement.

'You want me?'

'Oh no,' said Harry. 'I'm sorry. It's a Mr Vince Jardine I'm looking for.'

Even eight years ago there was no way this old man could have been up to helping relieve Fleet Television of half-a-million quid. He now put out a hand to the door-frame for support and stood eyeing Harry.

'You're after Vince?'

The old woman had reappeared behind the man so that they now both stood regarding him. He knew from their expressions there was something odd here.

'Does he not live here?' he asked.

'Not any more, no,' said the old woman quietly.

'He's dead, son,' said the old man. 'Been dead and buried two years now.'

'Two years and three days,' said the woman.

'I see,' said Harry, taken aback. 'I'm sorry.'

'Were you a mate of his or what?'

'Not, er, not really, no.'

He'd expected anything but this and now found it difficult to frame the questions he knew needed to be asked. How had Vince Jardine died? Under what circumstances? Had he received any disturbing letters shortly before his death?

'Well, I'm sorry you've had a wasted journey,' said the old man.

'Was it, er . . . sudden?' asked Harry.

It was the old woman who answered. 'Sudden enough. He was only thirty-five.'

'And here's us lived all this time,' said the old man. 'Dun't seem fair somehow, does it?'

Harry shook his head. 'I'm sorry,' he said. 'Sorry to have disturbed you.'

'Ah well,' said the old man with a sigh. 'You weren't to know. Good-day to you, then.'

And he closed the door.

Harry passed the postman on his way out.

'Did you find who you were after?'

'I found where he used to live.'

A helpful young man, the postman thought about it, then said, 'There might be his new address at the post office. That's if he's having his letters sent on.'

'I don't think he is,' said Harry. 'And if he were I doubt they'd ever get there.'

'But you're not doubting that he's actually dead?'

Harry hesitated only a moment. He remembered the faces of the old couple. You couldn't get actors like that, not even at the National.

110

'No,' he said, 'I'm not doubting that. I just want to know what he died of.'

'So why didn't you ask them?'

He sighed. No doubt the hardened investigator would have done; he hadn't been able to bring himself to push that old couple into talking about their son's death. No more than he could now explain that to Yvonne.

'I didn't think,' he said abruptly.

'So you'll want to see his death certificate, then, will you?'

He looked at her in surprise. 'Can you get it?'

'I can get a copy of it.'

'Another of Clifford's little contacts, is it?'

'No. Anybody can do it. We just apply to St Catherine's House on Kingsway. They'll send us a copy of any death certificate we want. Provided we send them ten pounds.'

'Oh, marvellous,' said Harry. 'Let's ask 'em, then.'

He was constantly surprised to find how much information there was lying around in directories and files and computers. The art lay in knowing where to look. An art in which, fortunately, Yvonne was a past master.

'So now it's just the two addresses we're after,' she said, unearthing the piece of paper on which he'd listed the names of the eight robbers. 'Frank Metcalf and Maurice Scanlon.'

'Looks like it.'

'Well, I did have a thought. What if I ask our contact in the police to run them through their computer and see if that comes up with anything? I assume they are the type of people who might have records?'

'Oh, they are,' admitted Harry. But he was uneasy about the idea: weren't there dangers in approaching the police, however unofficially? 'We wouldn't have to say

111

what we wanted the addresses for, would we?'

'No.'

'And suppose they ask?'

'Well, I can't tell them anything, can I? Since you still haven't told me what this business is all about.'

Harry hadn't wanted to seem over-eager and perhaps frighten Jill off and so had resisted for a day or two the urge to ring her and, instead, had started reading the book she'd lent him. It was, the blurb promised, 'a funny yet touching insight into the sexual politics of modern America' and was written by 'one of the country's outstanding literary talents'. So the contents came as something of a surprise to Harry, who might have been no critic but who had once run a dirty bookshop while its owner was in Amsterdam on a busman's holiday and who therefore knew hard porn when he came across it.

There was, he had to admit, rather more story than you'd get in the cellophane-wrapped publications that had been the speciality of the shop in which he'd worked, and the writing style was distinctly superior, offering passages of high-flown and exotic description with which, say, *Lesbian Frolics* couldn't compete. Which only meant more power to its elbow, rendering the description of sexual activities more powerful than anything in *Lesbian Frolics* could ever be.

It was a strange feeling to know Jill had read it before him. Stranger still to realise she'd obviously approved of it since why else would she have selected it for him?

In fact, it was a strange, new world altogether, this world of Miss Jill Hanscombe, with its polite, unblinking acceptance of sex and violence. Harry, who associated both with his working life rather than with entertainment, found it hard to take.

At least though the question of how long he should

wait before phoning her again was answered for him. He returned to the office to be told by Yvonne there'd been a message for him. Without further comment, she handed him a sheet from her note-pad on which she'd written: 'Miss Hanscombe called. Could you ring her back?'

'When was this?' said Harry, hoping he wasn't betraying too much of his surprise and pleasure.

'This afternoon. You were out. She said to tell you she'd be at home all evening.'

'Oh. Right. Thanks.'

He waited to return the call until he knew she'd have had time to get home from school. Which also meant Yvonne had finished for the day and so, conveniently, he had the office to himself. The phone was picked up on the second ring. This time he wasn't thrown by the way she waited silently for him to speak.

'Jill? It's me, Harry.'

'Oh, hi. How are you?'

'All right. Yvonne said that you rang.'

'Yes. Sorry if it disturbed anything but it'd never occurred to me until I wanted it that I haven't got your home number. And I couldn't find it in the book.'

'No, you wouldn't.'

'Why, you're ex-directory?'

'No. Just haven't got a phone, that's all.'

'Ah.' She obviously hadn't considered that possibility.

'But you can always get me here. Don't worry about that.'

'OK. Well, look, what I was ringing for – would you like to come to dinner on Saturday?'

'Love to,' he said quickly.

The two of them together for the evening with no plays to interrupt was a wonderful prospect. Doubly wonderful since the idea had come from her.

'Are you sure?'

'Course I'm sure,' he insisted, puzzled she should ask.

'No, I just got the impression you might be used to more exciting nights out than a dinner at home.'

Like what for goodness' sake? It was the most exciting thing he could imagine.

'No, I'd love to come.'

'Well, OK then. Say eight for eight-thirty?'

'Sure.'

'Well, I'll see you, then.' Which would have left him as happy as a sandboy till eight o'clock on Saturday had she not added: 'Oh, there'll be two more friends of mine, Tony and Diane. I'm sure you'll get on.'

'Oh.'

His disappointment must have been audible even over the phone, for she asked, 'Is that all right?'

'Oh yes, sure, great.' he said quickly.

'Oh good. Bye for now, then.' And she rang off.

Though he was still pleased by the prospect, the delight he'd felt when he'd imagined the two of them alone had taken a sharp nose-dive now Tony and Diane had suddenly barged their way into the picture. God knew who they were but it was a fair bet they'd be the arty-farty type who'd get their kicks from modern American novels rather than from *Lesbian Frolics*.

Meanwhile the Phil Holliday case had entered something of a limbo which made Harry wonder if he hadn't done all he could. Was this the point to throw in the towel – apologise to Phil and present him with his bill? After all, he'd undertaken no more than to track down as many of the original gang as he could in an attempt to find (a) whether anybody else had been the object of a blackmail threat, and (b) whether any of them could have been the blackmailer.

Of the eight original robbers, one had already been

murdered – Les Pinfield – and another – Phil Holliday – had hired him to conduct the investigation. Which had left him with six. Of those six he'd spoken to Ronnie Franks, Neil Patterson and Tommy Coyle but hadn't made much progress except to have excited the attentions of the driver of a blue Datsun. He'd discovered that Vince Jardine had been dead for two years and three days, though he didn't yet know the cause of that death or whether there might be anything suspicious about it. As for the last two gang-members on the list – Frank Metcalf and Maurice Scanlon – there was no sign.

Phil Holliday, now phoning him daily for news of any progress, had placed the West Ham badge in his shop window as instructed. Which, however, had so far produced no further communication from the blackmailer.

It wasn't only an unsatisfactory outcome to the case; it was also an unsatisfactory moment to leave it. He'd at least give it another day or two. Wait and see what Vince Jardine's death certificate might reveal.

He thought Yvonne was about to tell him precisely that when he entered the office the following morning and was greeted by her announcement: 'Progress at last.'

'Progress . . .?'

'With this silly case of yours that you won't tell me anything about.'

'Oh yes. What, you've got a copy of the death certificate, have you?'

'Oh no, that won't come till Monday. There's always a bit of a delay while they look for it. No, I've got you one of those last two addresses you wanted.'

'Oh good,' said Harry. 'Frank Metcalf?'

'No, the other one. Scanlon. It came via our contact in the police. But I don't know whether you're going to like it.'

'Like it?' said Harry, puzzled. 'How d'you mean?'

Yvonne gave him a smile that was half-sympathetic, half-amused. Clifford had filled her in on the story of Harry's past.

'He's in prison,' she said. 'Wormwood Scrubs.'

'He's not,' said Harry in disbelief.

'He is. And will be for a while yet. Burglary and possession of firearms. He got three years six months and he's about halfway through his sentence.' She waited as Harry got over the surprise, then she asked quietly, 'Do you still want to go and see him?'

Well, was there much point? Maurice Scanlon could hardly be responsible for blackmail and murder from inside the Scrubs. It was about as good an alibi as you could get. On the other hand . . . well, he had promised Phil Holliday he'd try and see *all* the other robbers, so it would be another loose end tied up.

And the thought of returning to the Scrubs – only this time not as an inmate but as an almost respectable sort-of-detective operating for once on the side of the angels – it was irresistible.

'Why not?' he said. 'See if you can arrange it.'

I get up that morning feeling sick to my stomach and can't touch any breakfast. Course Margie knows there's something going on and repeats what she's said before about me not seeing her or the kids again if I get nicked. Just the sort of encouragement I need really. We're all making our own way to Fleet and we all have different times to arrive so that we're going in in ones and twos and not mob-handed. Then by half-ten we meet up in the gents on the fourth floor. At least them that're doing the heavy business do. The drivers are doing their own thing making sure the cars are parked nice and handy. And then of course there's Tommy in the foyer with his bleeper. He's to give us three bleeps to tell us the van's arrived, two to tell us they're in the building and one that the lift's on its way. It must have looked like a queers' convention in that fourth-floor bog. Les is already there when I go in and then Vince and Frank arrive together. Every time anybody comes in we have to be combing our hair or washing our hands or having a pee – though you can only do so much of that to order. Ronnie has us worried, not turning up till there's only five or ten minutes to the off and Frank in particular is abusing him something rotten when all of a sudden he comes in through the door all hot and bothered and telling us about delays on the tube. But everybody shuts him up. The van should be here now and so we're all stood there listening for Frank's bleeper to bloody well bleep. Suppose it's not working says Les. We'll still be here this time tomorrow. So why didn't you have a better idea says Frank. And then fortunately somebody comes in to have a pee so we all have to start hair-combing and hand-washing again but at least the aggro has to stop. The guy has his pee while we're all keeping our faces turned the other way and then he goes out. Christ says Les, it's five minutes late. And Frank is looking at his bleeper and shaking it and holding it up to his ear but there's still nothing comes out of it. I feel so sick I'm going to need one of those lavatories for real in a minute. Why don't we just go out and see what's happening, says Vince. No says Les sticking by the plan, we've got to wait. And Frank opens up the back of the bleeper to check the batteries are in place. You know he wants to throw it out of the window but if he does that then we're all buggered.

IX

Full of good intentions to catch up on the paperwork that was fast becoming the bane of his life, Harry called in at the office on Saturday morning and thus picked up the newly-delivered envelope that had an embossed crest and the words 'St Catherine's House' decorating its flap.

Inside was a copy of Vince Jardine's death certificate. Scanning it quickly, Harry saw that Vincent Giles Jardine had died in the Intensive Care Ward of the London Hospital, Whitechapel, on 7th October 1983 and had been seen on that same day, both before and after death, by a medical practitioner with an illegible signature. The 'Cause of Death' section was subdivided into 'Disease or condition directly relating to death', 'Antecedent causes', and 'Other significant conditions'. In the case of Vincent Giles Jardine, the first had been 'Cerebral Haemorrhage', the second 'Sub-arachnoid Haemorrhage', and the third 'Coma'. It was a medical mumbo-jumbo that meant little to Harry except that it didn't seem to suggest a knife in the guts.

He went in search of Yvonne's dictionary and looked up 'Cerebral'. 'Of the brain,' it said. 'Sub-arachnoid' was more of a problem. The word didn't appear, though there was 'Arachnid' which the dictionary explained as 'Member of the class of animals including spiders, scorpions and mites.' 'Haemorrhage' sounded more familiar and, sure enough, that did appear: 'Bleeding, especially when extensive.'

119

So either Vince Jardine had bled to death after being attacked by spiders and scorpions – not all that common an occurrence in East London – or the word 'Arachnoid' really was nothing to do with 'Arachnid'. Harry decided to settle for the latter. He'd also settle for letting Yvonne uncover the true meaning of the phrase. Whatever it was, it didn't sound likely to bring him any nearer to Phil Holliday's blackmailer.

Was anything? Probably not, unless it was of the blackmailer's own choosing. Harry might go and see Maurice Scanlon in the Scrubs: he might continue in pursuit of the elusive Frank Metcalf; but he had little hope of either telling him anything he didn't know already. The real point and purpose was to provoke the blackmailer into coming after him again.

It wasn't the method he would have chosen. Setting himself up as an Aunt Sally had to be way beyond the call of duty. In fact you had to be some kind of nut to do it. In Harry's case, the pig-headed kind. The kind who told himself he'd never be able to look himself in the shaving-mirror again if he allowed himself to be scared off after coming this far.

No, he'd carry on a bit longer, at least till he met the scorpions and spiders face to face.

He arrived at 48 Ashley Road on the dot of eight o'clock, carrying a wrapped bottle of dry, white wine and wondering what the hell he was letting himself in for. Better murderers and blackmailers than this.

Jill opened the door to him looking lovelier than ever, with huge, gold ear-rings and her hair cut short. She stood on her tiptoes to kiss his cheek as he handed her the wine.

'I'm glad you could come,' she said.

'Try and stop me.'

Though it was a small disappointment to see the other

two guests already there before him. There was a man with a beard lounging on the sofa and a young woman with frizzy, red hair looking busy in the kitchen area. They were both casually dressed, making Harry feel formal in his collar and tie and three-piece.

'Now let me introduce everybody,' said Jill brightly. 'Harry, this is Diane and Tony.' And to them she said, 'This is Harry.'

'Nice to meet you, Harry,' said Tony, and they shook hands.

'Hi, Harry,' called Diane. 'I'll be with you in a sec, only these artichokes are getting a bit critical.'

'Have a drink,' said Jill. 'What would you like?'

He opted for lager and sat in a chair opposite Tony.

'Is it still raining?'

'No.'

'It was raining when we got here.'

'I've already told them what you do,' said Jill. 'Tony's a lecturer and Diane's a teacher.'

'I see,' said Harry, not exactly encouraged by the news but hardly surprised either. If villains tended to mix with villains then the probability was that teachers, too, stuck to their own kind.

'You come far?' asked Tony.

'Stepney,' said Harry, then explained how he'd come by tube after his car had let him down again, this time refusing to start altogether.

'Oh, but that's such an awful journey for you,' protested Jill. 'I didn't realise you hadn't the car.'

'At least he can drink without worrying about being breathalysed,' pointed out Tony.

'Where do you live?' asked Harry.

'Ealing. Always have. Funny, isn't it, how you get to regard an area of London as your own and couldn't ever imagine living anywhere else.'

'It is,' said Harry, wondering which area was his and

121

why it was he could happily contemplate living almost anywhere but where he invariably ended up.

'Rumour has it you're a private detective,' said Diane, leaving the artichokes and coming to join them.

Harry nodded.

'I once had a private detective trailing me.'

Tony gave a derisive laugh. It meant he recognised the story and didn't think it worth repeating.

'I did,' insisted Diane, and continued to Harry: 'It was when I was working as an au pair for this rich old bird in Golders Green. During the university vac. And she had me followed by this really seedy-looking man in a raincoat.'

'Sounds like a private detective,' said Harry solemnly.

'Oh sorry, no. I don't mean you're like that. But I mean he was. You see, she was totally neurotic, this woman I worked for. Thought everybody was stealing from her.'

'He was probably a flasher,' said Tony, yawning.

'So why did she sack me?'

'Because you attracted flashers. How the hell should I know?'

Harry took the opportunity of their dispute to move from his seat to where Jill, slightly flushed from the cooking, was doing last-minute things to the table.

'And how're you?'

'Oh, OK. At least I will be once everybody sits down and starts eating. It's such a bloody little kitchen for feeding more than one at a time.'

'I read some of that book you lent me.'

'What book?'

'The novel. The one that . . .'

'Oh yes, of course. Do you like it?'

'Sort of. I haven't got very far.'

She nodded and left it at that, being preoccupied with saucepans and plates. Feeling rebuffed, he rejoined Tony and Diane.

'Do you have much to do with our wonderful police force?' asked Tony.

'Not a lot, no.'

'Lucky you,' said Diane.

Harry shrugged.

'Be a police state in five years,' said Tony. 'You'll have to have identity papers to get from Stepney to here.'

'It's a police state already,' said Diane, finishing her drink.

'Oh, the structure's there and the techniques have been tried and tested,' agreed her husband (or boyfriend or whatever he was). 'Northern Ireland, the miners' strike – it's all been a godsend to the right wing of this country. Got us used to seeing riot-shields and plastic bullets. Got the command structure centralised. But they're not quite there yet. They're not quite ready to own up and say yes, this is what it's going to be like all the time. They're still playing at emergencies, pretending it's only temporary and that when things have changed we can all go back to Dixon of Dock Green again.'

'What do you lecture about?' asked Harry

'Politics and economics.'

'Oh.'

'We've also got this new department – Communication Studies – and I'm in on the ground floor of that.'

'Oh God,' groaned Diane; then called to Jill, 'It's Communication Studies already.'

'It's a field I'd really like to get into,' continued Tony, ignoring her. 'It's a fascinating area. The way the media manipulate people. All part of the same process of course. Control rather than consensus.'

'Stop being so boring,' said Jill, coming to them with more drinks. 'You'll have Harry leaving before we've started eating.'

'He never stops,' said Diane.

123

'Sorry,' muttered Tony, looking put out.

It should have been familiar to Harry, this moaning about the Old Bill and their methods but he couldn't help feeling that the villains from whom he'd been used to hearing it would have had little sympathy for Tony's fears of totalitarianism. If you were a villain you cursed the bent coppers for being bent and feared the unbent ones for not being. You didn't get het up about riot-shields and rubber bullets unless you could get a finger in the lucrative business of supplying them.

'Right, gang. Everybody to the trough,' announced Jill, and they moved to the table amid expressions of eager anticipation.

As well as the promised artichokes there was some sort of fish pâté and then beef and rice, with enough wine to start Tony talking again, this time about Third World economics and the decline of the West. Jill strove to make light of the subject, a couple of times inviting Harry to join her in deriding it, but he didn't feel up to much more than a grunt of agreement. He was happier left to concentrate on the food. His eating out had been among the numbered menus of Indian and Chinese restaurants. This was a richer and less familiar fare.

'Did you see that old Sinatra film on telly last night?' Jill asked, cutting across Tony's protestations that the Far East was set to become the new trading centre of the world.

'No,' said Harry. 'What was it?'

She shook her head. 'It doesn't matter. I can't remember the title now.'

'Main characteristic of television,' said Tony. 'Everything's instantly forgettable.'

'You could say that about most things,' said Jill.

'Especially men,' said Diane.

Tony groaned softly.

'Most men,' she went on, helping herself to another

124

glass of wine, 'think they're the world's greatest drivers
and the world's greatest lovers. In fact most of them
should stick to milk-floats and masturbation.'

'And you'd know, would you?'

'Not about milk-floats, no.'

'Will you be able to get your car fixed OK?' asked Jill,
turning to Harry.

'I'd better do. There's no way I can go on working
without it.'

'Basically women are looking for love, men for
pornography,' pronounced Diane.

'I suppose pornography's easier to find,' retaliated
Tony. 'And cheaper.'

'Depends where you're looking. A man's ideal
woman is a tart. Available, usable, disposable.'

Tony gave a small, hopeless laugh which his wife (or
girl-friend or whatever she was) seemed to take as an
admission of defeat, for she turned to Harry: 'Have you
ever been married, Harry?'

'Never.'

'And why not?'

'Oh, come on, Di,' broke in Jill. 'He doesn't have to
answer that.'

'No, but I thought he might want to.'

'And why might he? Nobody has to explain why
they're not married, for God's sake. Listening to you,
I'd have thought you were against the whole idea
anyway.'

'Hear, hear,' muttered Tony.

'I am. I wish I'd never got married, I can tell you
that.'

'Thank you,' muttered Tony.

(Husband and wife, then, thought Harry.)

'And what about you?' Diane continued to Jill. 'You
got out. You're surely never going to risk all that
again?'

125

'I would have thought,' said Harry, 'that nobody's all that keen on marriage. I mean as an idea. Till they meet somebody they want to get married to.'

There was a silence and he knew he must sound slow-witted and out of his depth. Their talk was to entertain, he realised, not to arrive at prosaic truths. He should have kept his mouth shut and left them to their twittering.

'Absolutely,' said Jill loyally.

'The trouble comes when you keep on meeting people you want to get married to,' said Diane, rallying, 'and you find you're still stuck with the first one.'

'Must be awful for you,' said Tony. 'Especially if he's a man. The last of the great minority groups.'

'Oh, you're after pity now?'

'It'd be an improvement on contempt.'

This time Harry let them get on with it and made no attempt to contribute. Jill left the table and bustled about, moving plates and providing coffee. Harry remained where he was as audience to the sparring of the other two.

'I just wish you'd married a real male chauvinist. Then you'd have something to complain about.'

'I did,' said Diane. 'And I am doing.' She turned to Jill. 'D'you mind if I smoke?'

Jill glanced at Harry before shaking her head and saying no, why should she?

The sudden display of proprieties surprised Harry, particularly when Diane asked him, 'You won't arrest me or anything, will you?'

'I've never arrested anybody in my life.'

'Oh, good.'

And she went to her bag and came back with a thickly-rolled wad of cannabis.

Harry's surprise must have shown, for she said, 'You thought I meant the king-size, filter-tip variety? Sorry.

Does that mean you will arrest me after all?'

'No.'

'That's nice of you. Do you smoke?'

She was offering him the joint. He shook his head. 'No, thanks.' So she offered it to Jill and there was a moment when Harry knew Jill would have taken it without a qualm had he not been there. 'Don't let me stop anybody else though,' he muttered. She took it and inhaled, then passed it on to Tony and went back to clearing the table.

The talk got round to religion. Diane reported on how she'd answered her door to find two Mormons waiting to convert her and had countered by trying to convert them to her atheism till they'd fled the unequal contest. Jill wondered why Americans were so susceptible to religion and was informed by Tony that, along with Walt Disney and Hollywood, it was a symptom of their national immaturity. Jill related how she'd failed in attempting to teach a James Joyce book to one of her classes because the kids had had no understanding of his sense of guilt.

Harry cleared his throat and said, 'Well, I'd better be going.'

It produced an immediate reaction that was itself near to guilt, as if they were all suddenly aware of how much they'd been neglecting him.

'Oh no . . .'

'Surely not yet? There are late tubes, aren't there?'

But he insisted, knowing he'd have nothing more to say to them if he stayed all night and wanting to escape the atmosphere which had become claustrophobic, not merely with the heavy scent of cannabis but with their talk from which he was excluded.

Still, there was one last question before he went.

'Does anybody know what a sub-arachnoid haemorrhage is?'

'Diane teaches biology,' said Tony eagerly.

'It's a sort of bleeding around the brain,' she said. 'In the brain tissue. Not very nice.'

'What causes it?'

'Might be anything. Might even be spontaneous.'

Not spiders, then. Not helping him towards Phil Holliday's blackmailer either. But at least he wasn't leaving completely empty-handed.

Jill went with him to the door.

'Sorry you haven't enjoyed yourself,' she said quietly.

'Who says I haven't?' he protested.

'Oh, come on. You looked like we were boring you to death most of the time.'

'I always look like that. Doesn't mean anything.'

'You made them nervous, you see. They don't normally go on like that, bitching at one another.'

He stared at her, taken aback by this new view of things: that it was they who'd been nervous about meeting him.

'No, I've enjoyed it,' he muttered. 'And thanks for inviting me.'

'See you again?'

'Yes,' he said. 'You can count on it.'

Feeling himself suddenly smiling, he realised how sullen and unresponsive he must have appeared. He must have seemed a slob-and-a-half. All the more wonderful of Jill to understand and forgive him.

He bent and kissed her lightly.

'Look after yourself,' she said.

'And you.'

She closed the door.

He left the house and headed for the tube, still angry with himself for his boorish performance. The whole evening had left him bitterly frustrated – with himself, with the fact he hadn't been able to talk to Jill, and with the sheer physical effort of sitting through the ordeal. He was glad to be out and walking.

Had he not been he might never have spotted the blue Datsun parked on the other side of the road.

It was, he was sure, the same blue Datsun that had followed him earlier. Even from a distance he could see the silver scratches on the wing where it had scraped the wall in escaping him.

He walked on, his heart pounding, until a tree gave him the cover he needed to stop and look back. The car seemed to be empty. He looked round quickly, fearful lest the driver were following him on foot, but he could see no-one. He crossed the road, then walked back until he was close enough to the car to reassure himself that it was indeed empty.

He re-crossed the road and came back to stand beneath the shadow of the tree. Taking out his note-book, he jotted down the car number – HBZ 329V. No way was he missing that again. Then he waited, reasoning with himself that the driver couldn't be far away and would soon be returning. Most probably he was again in pursuit of Harry and had this time parked a short distance away from Ashley Road so as not to be spotted and had gone in search of Harry's own car.

Which, as luck had it, Harry hadn't brought. So that it couldn't be long before his pursuer, failing to find any sign of Harry's car, would return to his own.

In fact, it was twelve minutes.

The streets were near enough deserted so that the sound of footsteps alerted Harry before he saw the figure of a man, hands thrust into pockets and shoulders hunched, coming down the other side of the road. Harry didn't recognise him. It wasn't one of the robbers he'd already met. Which meant it was either Frank Metcalf or somebody else not a member of the original

129

gang. There was, of course, still the chance he was an innocent passer-by. Harry waited for confirmation and got it when the man slowed and stopped beside the Datsun. There was the small jingle of car-keys.

This time there'd be no dramatic get-away. Harry sprinted forward, crossing the road and reaching the man before he'd had the chance to do more than raise his head in surprise.

Harry grabbed him by the throat and thrust him back against the car.

'You looking for me?'

'What . . .?'

'Well, now you've found me. So let's hear just what the hell you think you're playing at!'

The other man came to life, lashing out wildly with both hands and catching Harry across the side of the head.

Incensed by the blow – and anyway conscious of how Les Pinfield had lingered too long and ended up skewered on the end of a knife – Harry went into action. Letting go of the man's throat, he threw a volley of punches into his body that doubled him over, then hit him hard about the head, ending with an uppercut that brought a yell of pain. The man fell and lay gasping at Harry's feet.

It was the action he needed after the tortuous inactivity of the evening.

He stepped over the grunting body and felt the pockets, but there was no knife, at least none he could find. He stepped back.

The other man moved as though to get to his feet, but failed and flopped back against the side of the car. The noise of their scuffle seemed to have gone unnoticed. The street was still deserted.

'OK, pal,' said Harry, 'so let's hear it. Just who the hell are you?'

The other man swore inaudibly. There was blood pouring from his nose, already covering the front of his shirt.

'I said who are you!'

He grabbed him and pulled him upright.

'You should know,' said the man, grimacing with pain.

'I should know a lot of things. Things you're going to tell me.'

'Bastard.'

'Maybe. But what about you? Where do you fit in?'

'You want to know who I am?'

'You've got it.'

This time he had to spit out a mouthful of blood before speaking.

'I'm nobody, me. I'm just the poor sod whose wife you've been knocking off.'

'What the hell are you on about?'

Even as he asked, he knew the answer and his heart dropped.

'My wife,' repeated the man dully.

'Oh yes? And who's she, then?'

His bluster must have shown for what it was. The man managed a sickly grin.

'Jill Hanscombe. Or at least I believe that's what she's gone back to calling herself.'

Harry let go of him and stepped back.

'She's not your wife,' he said weakly.

'Still is as far as I'm concerned,' said the man, raising a tentative hand to his swollen and bloody nose. 'Still would be if it weren't for bastards like you.'

'Is that why you were following me the other night?' asked Harry flatly.

'I try and keep an eye on her. See she comes to no harm.'

'I thought you were somebody else.'

The man gave a bitter laugh, then winced as the pain caught up with him.

Harry bent, retrieved the other man's car-keys from where they'd fallen and handed them to him.

'I'm sorry.'

The man laughed again.

'I am. I thought you were somebody else.'

'Piss off.'

Harry could only stand and watch as Jill's ex-husband tried with trembling fingers to fit the key into the car-door. He finally managed it and climbed in.

'You shouldn't have followed me like that,' said Harry.

'And you shouldn't have been messing with my wife.'

The car-door was slammed closed, then he was off, accelerating away down the street.

Harry groaned aloud. It wasn't the first time he'd been too quick with his fists but he had seldom regretted it so bitterly. How in God's name had he come to do a thing like that – to have beaten up Jill's ex-husband even as he was coming away from her flat after a civilised evening with her joint-smoking friends?

He started to walk slowly down the street, still too dismayed by the turn of events to take in fully what they might mean or what might be the price he'd have to pay. Till he was surprised by the now unmistakable sound of the Datsun engine. The car was returning, coming back along the street. It went past him, reached the end and turned left. It was retracing the path by which he'd come from Ashley Road.

Of course. He wasn't going to the police or to a solicitor. Though either of those might come later. First, battered and bloody as he was, he was going to see Jill. Or rather to let her see him. Let her see the damage her boy-friend had done and leave her to draw her own conclusions.

Harry thought for a moment of pursuing him, of turning up on the doorstep alongside him, but it would have been futile. Nothing he could have said – apologies, explanations – could have matched the brutal testimony to his own savagery that the other man bore for all to see.

He went on towards the tube, sick and furious at the way events had betrayed him.

The bleeper bleeps three times and Frank's so surprised he drops it on the floor. About bleeding time says Vince. Oh God says Ronnie. And we all feel this great relief because it's happening at last but there's still part of you wishes it wasn't. It's like going over the top out of the trenches and in ten minutes you'll either be dead or bloody heroes. Or in our case either nicked or bloody rich. Come on says Frank, and we go out of that bog door and down the corridor at a trot. There's nobody there to see us till we turn the corner and then there's the two blokes from the cash office just where they should be standing by the lift talking. They both look round as we arrive and one starts to grin as if he's expecting a joke but then Frank waves a piece of lead piping under their noses and says, One word and you get this. The rest of us push 'em up against the wall and lash their wrists together with sticky tape and then stick some more across their mouths. But making sure their noses aren't covered 'cause we don't want two stiffs. One starts to struggle and Vince hits him across the neck with half a pickaxe handle he's produced from under his jacket. Les has an old wooden truncheon and Ronnie a monkey wrench. I've brought an iron bar that's proved its use in the past and that's as much a mascot as a weapon. Then Les unlocks the store-room door and we shove 'em both in. Another wait then the bleeper goes twice telling us they've brought the cash inside and are loading it into the lift. Which means we're ahead of ourselves and now have to stand around feeling conspicuous. It's Les who thinks of it. Get in there he says, meaning the store-room. So we all crowd in, more or less treading on the two who're already in there all trussed up. The one who's conscious looks scared to death thinking we're going to do for him I suppose, but we just stand there keeping quiet especially when somebody walks past. Then the bleeper goes once, meaning they're on their way up. Out again says Les, and we all pile out of the store-room and face the lift doors.

X

There were odd moments of optimism when he wondered whether Jill might actually have welcomed the beating-up he'd given her husband. After all, if he'd been pestering her and refusing to accept the break-up of their marriage, wasn't there a chance she'd thank Harry for applying a little none-too-friendly persuasion?

Then the moment of optimism would be over, reality would intervene, and he'd have to recognise the truth: there was about as much chance of Jill Hanscombe applauding what he'd done as there was of a litter of pigs starting up their own airline. Jill Hanscombe resided in those gentler reaches of society where disputes were settled in court by way of words and not in the street by way of boots and fists. Harry had once known the wife of a betting-shop owner who, drunk and sporting a shining black eye, had offered him fifty pounds to break her husband's arm but probably even she hadn't been serious. Any such eye-for-eye stuff would strike Jill as barbaric. She'd despise him – would perhaps even fear him – for what he'd done.

Things, anyway, couldn't be left as they were. The following day, Sunday, he had a lunchtime drink, and then another, and then went to the office where he could use the phone.

Seeing the place outside of working-hours, it struck him as seedy and depressing. It was unheated and silent; in need of redecoration and refurnishing; after which it'd still be a dump.

Harry dialled her number and waited, not knowing

whether he wanted her to answer or not. Then the phone at the other end was lifted and there was the customary silence, one that he suddenly understood: not only did her ex-husband hang around outside her flat but he must also have kept calling her, wanting to talk.

'It's me,' he said. 'Harry.'

'Oh.'

Brief but to the point. That single, disparaging 'Oh' meant she'd seen the mess he'd made of her ex-husband and hated him for it.

'I suppose you heard about what happened last night?'

'Yes.'

'You want to hear my side of it?'

There was no reply, which he took as an invitation, and went on to explain how he'd known he was being followed but not by whom, how he'd had a previous encounter with a blue Datsun, and how he'd never had the slightest idea and could never have had the slightest idea that the man had anything to do with Jill.

'He doesn't,' she said. 'Not any more.'

'He seems to think he does.'

'Harry, I'm not interested in talking to you or to anybody else about my marriage. And I'm quite ready to believe that what happened last night was an accident.'

The words might have held out a promise of forgiveness but for the tone: there was an ominous flatness to the way she spoke that told him he'd had it. Like a judge summing up, she was ready to allow some slight mitigating circumstances, but she'd end by delivering a swingeing sentence.

'But I still think that what you did was awful. I mean I know you mix with some pretty violent people but, well, I suppose I fooled myself into thinking you might be different. But, after this . . . well, I can't fool myself any longer, can I?'

There was a pause. Harry toyed with 'Yes', then with 'No', but neither seemed appropriate. Then she continued.

'Anyway, I don't think we should meet again. And I'm sorry, I am. But if that kind of behaviour is what comes naturally to you then I just think we have nothing in common. Nothing.'

It wasn't a surprise except in how much it seemed to matter. God, he'd only seen the woman three or four times and they hadn't exactly been nights to remember. He still felt he was being unfairly blamed – anybody playing her ex-husband's stupid games was asking for trouble and he'd got it – but he wasn't going to give her the satisfaction of pleading his case or embarking on some pathetic apology.

'Suit yourself,' he said, and put down the receiver.

At least it freed him to get back to some sort of normal social life, which meant clubbing it in one of his old haunts till the small hours and then escorting home Miss Cheryl McPherson, who was also one of his old haunts.

Cheryl was a one-time croupier and brunette, now a barmaid and blonde. She lived in a tiny flat, full of soft toys and with postcards from foreign parts pinned up around the walls. She switched on the two-bar electric fire and poured a couple of large whiskies from a leather-clad decanter.

'I'll just go and get changed,' she said. 'You make yourself cosy.'

Harry took off his jacket marvelling that, with birds like Cheryl around, he'd ever bothered chasing after screwed-up English teachers who wouldn't know a good time if it stared them in the face. Literature had a lot to answer for. The only books in Cheryl's flat were a telephone directory and a photograph album of the royal wedding.

'Shan't be long,' came a call from the bedroom.

'No hurry.'

He meant it, too, feeling pleasantly cocooned and contented and wondering why all life couldn't be like this. Though, even in the midst of these musings, he had a sudden and uneasy sense of something still amiss. It was the telephone-call, the one he'd had at the office that'd warned him to stop asking questions about Les Pinfield if he valued his health. Now that hadn't come from Jill's ex. Whoever had made that call was still out there somewhere, watching and waiting.

He looked at Cheryl's phone which, reassuringly, was in the shape of a Mickey Mouse. Cheryl herself came back in a black, see-through baby-doll outfit.

'How do I look?'

'Fantastic.'

She looked at herself in the mirror, trying out different poses.

'I used to have a good figure once.'

'You still do.'

'Then how come I only see you once every blue moon?'

'That's what I keep wondering. I must be crazy.'

'You must.'

He left an hour later from a room made stiflingly hot by their passion and the two-bar electric fire. Outside it was cool and the streets deserted. There were no distraught husbands to accost him as he walked homeward. Not a word had been said all evening about the theatre, feminism or Third World economics.

'You've seen this death certificate for Vince Jardine, have you?' asked Yvonne.

'Yes.'

'Any use?'

'Depends on what you call use. It says he died of natural causes.'

138

'Haemorrhage,' read Yvonne. 'Sub-arachnoid haemorrhage.'

'I know.'

'I'll file it, shall I?'

'Might as well.'

She watched him, then asked, 'Do you still want me to arrange this prison visit?'

Harry hesitated. 'I don't know. Let me think about it.'

The agency was now busy again. The lean spell that had followed Clifford's death seemed to have run its course and there was now a steady demand for Harry's time, mostly process-serving and routine enquiries, with just the odd weird and wonderful client who was more often in need of a psychiatrist than a private detective. However, any wishful thoughts Harry might have been harbouring – that the Phil Holliday case would simply grind to a halt and be allowed to remain there – were disturbed by Phil himself who rang regularly once a day in need of reassurance and demanding news of progress.

'Have you heard any more from the blackmailer?' Harry countered.

'No.'

'Well, then. Perhaps we've scared him off.'

'Harry, I don't want him scaring off. I want to know who he is.'

'I told you I wasn't making any promises.'

Which point Phil would side-step with the question: 'Who're you going to see next?'

'Well, there's only two more on the list. As you well know.'

'Scanlon and Metcalf.'

'Right.'

'So who're you going to see first?'

'Well, I can't go and see Metcalf 'cause I don't know where the hell he is, do I? And neither does anybody else from what I can gather.'

139

'So Scanlon, then.'

'He's in the nick.'

'So you said. But you're still going to go and see him, aren't you?'

'That's not really up to me, is it?' said Harry evasively. 'The point is – does he want to see me? Because if he says no, then there's no way I can get to him.'

In fact, though, he said yes. He said it in a letter that arrived on Yvonne's desk and had come from the Governor's office, Her Majesty's Prison, Wormwood Scrubs. It stated that prisoner N37491 Scanlon had agreed to Mr Sommer's request to see him and enclosed a visiting-order for the following Saturday afternoon. Harry examined both letter and visiting-order with interest. They were not only contact with his past but proof that he'd graduated from Category C to the category of human being. The prospect of a return visit was irresistible even if he hadn't had Phil Holliday snapping at his heels.

'You're going to go, then?' asked Yvonne.

'I think I'd better. They might be putting on a special welcome for me.'

'And so they should.' Then she said, 'By the way, you still haven't told me what this case is all about, you know.'

'No,' he said, surprised it should still rankle.

'It's just that Clifford – Mr Humphries – often used to discuss cases with me. Even during our out-of-office rendezvous. And I like to think my advice might sometimes have been of help.'

'I'm sure it was. And if I want some help then I'll give you a shout. And that's a promise.'

In truth, he wouldn't have minded the chance to talk things over with her. The longer they worked together, the more he appreciated how much the past success of

140

the agency rested on her knowledge and good sense almost as much as on Clifford's unflagging energy. However, he still felt himself bound by his promise to Phil. He also feared how Yvonne would react if he ever did tell her. She'd surely be horrified to learn how he'd committed their slender resources to solving murder and blackmail.

Harry had never returned to the school from which he'd been expelled at the age of fifteen so that ringing the visitors' bell on the main gate of Wormwood Scrubs was the closest he'd been to the feeling of revisiting his alma mater. It was a strange feeling, too, this voluntary return to the prison in which he hadn't been particularly miserable, just held in a sort of clammy limbo till normal life could begin again.

He showed his visiting-order to a prison officer he didn't recognise and had his name and the purpose of his visit recorded. Then the door was relocked behind him and he was led across an inner courtyard and into a waiting-room. He couldn't see anything of E Wing, where he'd spent most of his time, but already there were familiar sounds and smells to make him uneasy. Above all, there was the unending succession of distant doors being slammed shut; their retorts carried back and forth along the galleries of cells.

Another prison officer arrived, one whom this time Harry vaguely recognised but who didn't seem to recognise him.

'You come to see prisoner N37491 Scanlon?'

'Yes.'

'This way please.'

And he led him along a corridor and up a small flight of steps, then held open a door for Harry to go through. The intermittent barrage of slammed doors continued in the middle distance but the smell of the place came to

141

meet them. It was a distillation of men in too close confinement overlaid with disinfectant. Harry gave a small shudder: he'd reckoned on confronting his past in the occasional nod of acknowledgement if at all; not in this faint reptilian stench to which he'd once contributed.

It was a small shock to find they were in the visiting-room. Harry knew it well, with its yellow, gloss-painted walls and its tables with partitions, but he'd always before entered it by a different door, one that led back into the maze of cells beyond. He'd come, embarrassed and awkward, to face his parents or his solicitor or the odd girl-friend or brother. Like everybody else, he'd looked forward to these grotesque encounters, then found them difficult and upsetting when they arrived. The dull routine of prison life acted as an anaesthetic; visits provided a painful jolt, reminding you of what you were missing.

'Half-an-hour,' muttered the prison officer as he brought Maurice Scanlon to sit in the canvas chair facing Harry.

Harry nodded to him, and N37491 Scanlon nodded back. He was younger than Harry had expected, no more than thirty, with longish hair and gaunt features.

The prison officer moved away. As a Category C prisoner, Scanlon was entitled to private conversation with his visitors. Though there wasn't, as yet, much conversation going on. Scanlon sat, defensive and curious, waiting to hear why Harry had come, while Harry wondered how to start telling him.

'Thanks for agreeing to see me.'

'No sweat. What's it about?'

'I'm a private detective and I'm here on behalf of a client of mine who's being blackmailed.'

Scanlon smiled. 'And you think I'm doing it?'

'No,' said Harry, returning the smile. 'I don't think

142

there's much chance of that.'

'So?'

'Look, the first thing I want to make clear – anything you tell me is in complete confidence. I mean I'm not the law. I'm not anything official. In fact it's not all that long ago I was sitting where you are listening to my brief telling me he'd done all he could.'

'What, you was doing time, was you?'

'More than once.'

It amused Scanlon, as Harry had hoped it would.

'What wing was you on?'

Harry told him, and they spent ten minutes talking about mutual acquaintances and bemoaning the food and cursing one of the screws who, Scanlon confirmed, was still as big a bastard as when Harry had known him. Naturally talkative, Scanlon was delighted at the chance to pass on some prison gossip to an old-timer out of touch. Harry was entertained and let him run on. Then, once he judged he'd established himself as kosher in the other man's book, he tried to direct him back to the matter in hand.

'You remember Phil Holliday . . .?'

'Phil . . . yeah.'

'And Les Pinfield and Ronnie Franks that you and some others worked with on a job about, oh, seven or eight years ago now . . .?'

'The Fleet telly job?'

'That's the one.'

And he told him about Les Pinfield's death, of which he'd already heard, and about the blackmail letters, of which he clearly hadn't, and of his own search for the members of the scattered gang.

'Can you think of anybody – apart from the eight of you – who might have had an inkling of what was going on?'

Scanlon shook his head firmly. 'No. That was what

143

was so good about it, see. We was all sworn to say nothing to nobody and then not even to see one another again afterwards.'

'That's what I've been hearing.'

'Well, it's the truth. And we stuck by it, didn't we? Oh, I know I'm banged up in here but that's 'cause I got careless. It wasn't anything to do with the Fleet job. Nobody's ever been done for that.'

They all said the same. Even took a shared pride in that they'd done what most villains only talked about – the one-off job with everybody taking his cut and then disappearing back into the trees.

'Fair enough,' said Harry. 'But how did you manage it? I mean there's always somebody talks, isn't there? Always somebody.'

'Not on this one there wasn't.'

'Why not?'

'Well, what it was, a lot of them involved was wanting out. I mean they was all older than me and they were thinking that they'd pushed their luck long enough and it was time for retirement.'

'Yes.'

'And then the job was clever. I mean there's no denying that. There was a lot of planning and everybody pulling their weight and so you thought from early on well, maybe this one is a bit different. Maybe for once it's going to be just like in the films.'

'But that's when people start talking, isn't it? When they want to show off and tell their mates all about how clever they've been?'

Scanlon shook his head. 'Wouldn't have dared.'

'No?'

'For one thing we was all sworn, you see. Oh, not like signing documents and that but there was a meeting early on where Frank – Frank Metcalf . . .'

The ever-elusive Frank Metcalf, thought Harry, and nodded.

144

'Well, he got us all to agree that if anybody talked, if it was ever found that anybody had been grassing on the rest of us, then he'd be for the chop. That the rest of us would do for him.'

'Kill him?'

Scanlon shrugged. 'Kill him, yeah.'

'And so that's why nobody's ever said a word.'

'I should think so, yeah. See, there might have been some that would never have gone through with it – I mean with actual killing – but there was some that would.'

'Who?'

'Well, Frank for starters. You haven't met Frank yet, have you?'

Harry shook his head.

'Well, he's one to be reckoned with is Frank. And then there was Neil. Another nutter on his day. And the other blokes I didn't know all that well but I mean generally there was the feeling that if any one of us stepped out of line then the other seven would sort him.'

It was a new insight into the workings of the gang, this revelation of the threat of extermination to back up the camaraderie that had kept them true to one another. Something none of the others had seen fit to mention, not even Phil who was supposed to be on Harry's side if anybody was. It'd taken the Scrubs' old boys' network to let him in on the secret.

Not that it pointed him to his blackmailer and murderer. But it did suggest a climate of violence that would have been a more likely spawning ground for both.

He decided to try Scanlon on the one suggestion of trouble that had come out of his interviews with the others.

'I believe you had a meeting the night before the job?'

'Yes.'

145

'There was something up, was there?'

For the first time Scanlon hesitated. He eyed Harry warily.

'Was there?'

'So I've been told.'

'And did anybody tell you what it was?'

'I was hoping you would.'

'Meaning nobody has.'

'Well, they probably have. I've just forgotten some of the details. So why don't you remind me of them?'

But he wasn't going to. Just smiled and slowly shook his head.

'Somebody got cold feet . . .?' prompted Harry.

'Did they?'

'Yes. Must have done.'

'If you say so.'

Where before they'd chatted on like old mates, here they were suddenly at loggerheads.

'I got the impression that there was something special,' said Harry patiently, 'that that last meeting was called for some specific reason . . .?'

Scanlon sat back in his chair. 'Sorry, boss. Can't help you.'

And, try as Harry may, he wasn't going to. Whatever had taken place at that final meeting, even Harry's credentials as an old boy of the Scrubs weren't enough to gain him admission to it.

'Somebody wanted out – was that it?'

Seeing he was guessing, Scanlon only shook his head. He'd said as much as he was ever going to say. The oath they'd taken binding them to silence evidently still held some of its power.

It puzzled Harry, though, that this man who'd talked so freely about his part in a major robbery should clam up on this one point. What extra and damning ingredient could this last-minute meeting have held that he wouldn't talk about it? Was there a seed sown here that, eight years later, had left Les Pinfield dead outside his own front door and Phil Holliday scared witless that he might follow suit?

'Why not tell me?' urged Harry. 'I know about the robbery. I could land everybody in it if I'd half a mind to. What would it change if I knew what happened at that one single meeting?'

Scanlon shook his head. He began to glance around him, as if the interview were already over. Which it very nearly was. They were running out of time. The prison officer who'd been keeping a distant eye on them was beginning to stretch and yawn, preparatory to moving in and announcing full-time.

'Anything I can do for you?' asked Harry, accepting he wasn't going to get any more and feeling he owed the other man a favour for what he'd got already. 'Messages or anything?'

'You got any fags?'

'Sure.'

He knew better than to enter onto the foreign soil of Her Majesty's prisons without a supply of its basic currency in his pocket and now managed a quick transfer to Scanlon on the blind side of the prison officer.

'Cheers.'

'How long have you left to do?'

'Year and seven months.'

'Any plans for when you get out?'

'Not yet. Oh, excepting to do with birds and booze. I got lots of plans for them.'

Harry laughed. The prison officer got to his feet and was watching as the second hand of the clock counted the visit to a close.

'I don't suppose you know where I can find Frank Metcalf?' asked Harry forlornly.

147

'Frank, yeah. Course I do.'

It was such a surprise Harry could only stare.

'Only, like I say, he's a hard man is Frank. I'd be very careful how you handle him.'

The prison officer was coming towards them.

'Where though?' asked Harry quickly.

'He's got a boozer. On the Seven Sisters Road. It's called the Three Musketeers. Dirty big place it is. You can't miss it. Only do me a favour, eh?'

'What?'

'Don't tell him I sent you.'

What we expect to see when the lift doors open is two security guards and a trolley full of money. What we don't expect is a dolly-bird with blonde hair down to her waist and legs that come up to meet it. She's got this big smile on her that just sort of freezes slightly when she sees what must have looked like the charge of the heavy brigade and her right in its path. I mean what must have happened – you can see it – these two security blokes have seen this dolly-bird waiting for the lifts. One look at her tits and all the instruction manual and years of training go out the window and they say here we are darling, come and have a ride with us. Not knowing that we're waiting on the fourth floor to bash their brains out. So for a split second nobody moves. 'Cause we're looking at the dolly-bird and she's looking at us and it gives her two boy-friends in crash-hats time to put their act together and one of 'em goes for the alarm button on the side of the lift while the other's fumbling with this truncheon he's got fastened to his belt. And then Frank lets out a yell and the magic moment's over and all hell's let loose. I manage to swing the old iron bar and catch the bloke going for the alarm button across his knuckles. Les grabs the bird and gets his hand over her mouth while she's still taking a deep breath preparatory to screaming her head off, and Ronnie, Vince and Frank come piling past me to have a go at guard number two who's got his truncheon off his belt at last but doesn't seem too sure what to do with it and while he's trying to make up his mind he gets cracked in all sorts of places where his crash-hat's not going to help him. Get 'em out of here, yells Frank. 'Cause it's like rush-hour conditions inside that lift with arms flailing about and this pile of money in the middle for us all to fall over. So we drag 'em out. The bloke I hit's holding his hand like it's extremely painful, which it probably is, so he's even more unhappy when I pull it behind his back and strap his wrists together. His helmet I leave on. It's better than a gag, what with the visor and all, he could scream blue murder and only deafen himself. The other guard who looks like he doesn't want to know anyway has been

149

trussed up and now we open up the old store-room again and heave 'em in. Come on then, says Les, meaning help him with the tart 'cause the two of them are still squirming about on the floor like they're having it away and all he's managing to do, Les, is keep his hand over her mouth so she can't yell. Anyway no shortage of volunteers and we strap her up. Les lets go of her mouth and quick as a flash Vince sticks a lump of plaster across it. Then she's into the store-room with the rest and the door's locked. Look at what the bitch did, says Les, and holds out his hand so we can see where she's bitten him. Come on, says Frank and we all squash into the lift around the money and I'm nearest the door so I press the button for the bottom floor and nothing happens.

XI

The Three Musketeers was every bit as big and every bit
as dirty as Maurice Scanlon had promised. The main bar
was an echoing vault of a room with seating running
around the walls and with a pool table at one end. The
décor was mustard-coloured and the carpets non-
existent. It was a place somehow overlooked in the
brewers' spending-spree that had updated most pubs
from male drinking-halls to lounge bars where you
could take the missus, and it therefore attracted the sort
of clientele that wouldn't want to take the missus
anyway: the hard-bitten drinkers, unemployed youths
and a small coterie of tarts, made-up and bejewelled in
defiance of their drab surroundings.

Harry went there on a lunchtime. If Frank Metcalf
were the hard man his reputation promised, he was
probably best tackled before rather than after dark. And
tackled sooner or later he had to be. Having come this
far and located seven of the robbers, there was no way
Harry could stop short of meeting the eighth. He didn't
any more expect to learn much but at least he'd feel he'd
seen the job through to its bitter end.

He ordered a pint of lager from a small, unshaven
man in shirt sleeves who was serving behind the bar and
who had the unmistakable air of being the hired help
and not the landlord.

'Frank Metcalf around?' he asked casually as he
received his change.

'Just popped out. He'll be in later.'

Harry nodded. 'Cheers.' He took his drink and found a seat that gave him a view of the bar and anything going on.

It wasn't a pub that enjoyed much of a lunchtime rush. Few of its customers looked capable of staging a rush of any kind except for a noisy group of youths who were on the pool table and having difficulty stopping the balls jumping off, at which there'd be a shout of laughter.

Harry quickly grew bored of staring around him and wished he'd a newspaper to pass the time, then remembered the book he was carrying in his pocket. He'd brought it to read during what promised to be a tedious afternoon keeping watch on a house in Plaistow at the request of the owner who wanted to know what his wife was getting up to in the afternoons. The book was the one Jill Hanscombe had lent him, the American novel that hovered between literature and depravity and that he still hadn't got more than halfway through.

He took it out now and started to read, though being careful to keep it on his lap where it was out of sight and wouldn't identify him as an eccentric. It was amusingly written and, under other circumstances, might have been mildly erotic. It dealt with the lives and loves of two New Yorkers who shared a marriage, a voracious appetite for sexual experimentation and a weakness for bouts of anguished introspection and self-doubt. There wasn't much in the way of a story.

There was a burst of laughter, then something hit Harry's foot. He saw that it was a chequered ball from the pool table and gave it a kick back in the direction of a close-cropped youth who was ambling towards him in pursuit.

As he did so, the door of the pub opened and Frank Metcalf entered. He was a heavily-built man with a balding head and black moustache but it was his air of

152

being on his own territory that identified him for Harry even before he raised the flap of the bar and went through.

Ah well, thought Harry, here goes.

He returned the book to his pocket, picked up his glass and walked over to the bar. Behind it, Frank Metcalf was talking to the barman who must have been telling him of Harry's enquiry for he turned and looked in Harry's direction. Though he didn't immediately come to speak to him. He first pulled himself a large whisky and added a splash of soda, and only then did he step across to where Harry was waiting.

'You were looking for me?'

'Frank Metcalf?'

A small nod, then: 'Who're you?'

'Harry Sommers,' said Harry, and placed one of the agency's printed cards down on the bar top for Metcalf to read. He'd considered what might be the best approach to this man, the last of the eight robbers, and had decided to revert to his earlier ploy of claiming he was working, not for Phil Holliday, but for Mrs Pinfield. Otherwise he'd play it straight. Tell Metcalf what he knew already and ask him the things he wanted to know.

There was a small crash as another ball shot from the pool table. Metcalf looked up quickly.

The laughter that had accompanied the ball's flight died. One of the youths hurried to retrieve the ball and the game recommenced but now without the shouting and fooling.

Metcalf turned back to Harry and his card.

'Private detective . . .?'

'Yes.'

'We don't get many of them in here. So, what can I do you for?'

'I'm making enquiries on behalf of a client, a Mrs

153

Pinfield.' When Metcalf didn't respond, he added, 'Les Pinfield's widow.'

It took another moment for Metcalf to locate the name.

'Les Pinfield . . .?'

'You once worked with him.'

'Did I, now?'

''Bout eight years ago.'

'You seem to know so much, what do you want to talk to me for?'

'Les Pinfield was murdered. And Mrs Pinfield thinks his death might have had something to do with the job you did together.'

Metcalf eyed him. It was a look that made Harry understand why the youths at the pool table were now playing quietly and carefully. He braced himself for what might be to come, then saw that Metcalf was smiling.

'Look, Mr . . .'

'Sommers.'

'Why don't we go and sit down to talk about this? I'm not in the habit of letting the whole world know my business.'

It seemed a reasonable suggestion and even to hold out hope that Metcalf might be helpful after all. Nevertheless, Harry would have preferred staying where he was. There was something about the landlord of the Three Musketeers he didn't trust. It wasn't just Maurice Scanlon's warning; his instincts told him that this was one of nature's heavies and was to be approached with caution.

'Sit down where?'

'Oh, just through in the other bar there.'

And he nodded towards a door that had the word 'Snug' engraved on it.

It looked safe enough. At least it was still in the public

domain where anyone could walk in.

'Whatever you say. It's your pub.'

Metcalf came from behind the bar and they went together into the Snug, which turned out to be much smaller and even scruffier than the main bar.

It was also occupied. A man wearing a donkey jacket was alone in a corner poring over a newspaper. He looked up as they entered.

'If you don't mind, Jimmy,' said Metcalf. 'Only this is private.'

The man didn't need telling twice. He made a quick gesture of deference, gathered up his newspaper and scuttled out.

'Sit down, Mr, er . . .'

'Sommers.'

They sat on opposite sides of a small table whose top was marked by beer-rings and cigarette burns. There was a short stretch of bar to Harry's left; otherwise the room was enclosed, with just the one door.

'So you reckon I worked with Les Pinfield, then?'

'Yes.'

'Go on. I'm interested.'

'There were eight of you did Fleet Television for half-a-million quid. And now Les has been killed. And another member of the gang has had a letter suggesting he might end up the same way.'

'Sounds nasty.'

'It is.'

'So where do I come into this?'

'Well, have you had anybody approach you? Anything that might have looked like an attempt at blackmail?'

'Not till now.'

Harry gave a small smile. 'You haven't, then?' he asked patiently.

'If I had, I can promise you one thing – they wouldn't

155

do it twice.'

Harry nodded, happy to let him play the hard man –
which he probably was – then went on, treading
carefully: 'Of course I'm not interested in the robbery.
That's nothing to do with me. But can I ask you on Mrs
Pinfield's behalf – can you think of anybody who might
have had a reason for wanting to kill her husband?'

Metcalf picked up his glass and drained it.

'Difficult question is that. Let me get you another
drink while I consider it.'

'I'm all right with this one, thanks.'

'Well, I'm not.' He got to his feet. 'I'll just get a refill.
And then see if I can't help you.'

And he left the room without a backward look. Harry
leant back in his chair, which gave him a view over the
bar. Metcalf reappeared on the other side of it and went
to refill his glass while saying something to the barman.

Harry had spent enough of his life in pubs and clubs
to know a dodgy situation when he saw one, especially
when he himself was in it. He'd showed his hand and
got nothing in return. And now here he was, left high
and dry, waiting helplessly for whatever might be about
to happen.

The unshaven barman appeared and held out a glass
which Harry had to rise to take.

'Compliments of the house.'

It was a large whisky.

Harry shrugged and took it. 'Thanks.'

'Mr Metcalf'll be with you in a minute.'

Harry looked past him and saw that Metcalf had
disappeared. He took the drink and went and sat down
again. Apparently satisfied, the barman retreated. Leaving Harry to do some quick thinking.

It was possible – just – that Metcalf would come back,
sit down and do his level best to help Harry all he could.
And that all he was doing at the moment was having a

pee, something he'd been too much of a gentleman to mention. It was also possible – much more so – that he'd no intention of giving Harry anything more than a drink on the house to keep him where he was while he'd slipped to the back to phone for assistance. And, when that assistance arrived, the small Snug with its privacy and its single door would be the scene of Harry's last stand.

A strategic retreat was called for. And fast. He took another look along the bar. There was still no sign of Metcalf. He moved to the door of the Snug and opened it. The yobbos, the tarts and the drinkers were all as before with no-one seeming to pay him any particular attention. He made a bee-line for the door. No-one shouted or moved to stop him. Within seconds, he was outside and walking briskly away.

The doubts began almost as soon as he hit the fresh air.

Had he really been in danger? What had Metcalf done or said that'd come anywhere near being a threat? He'd been reluctant to answer questions certainly; but that was understandable, as was his wish for their conversation to be in private.

Harry stopped and looked back at the door of the pub. An old man with a dog went in but no-one came out. His doubts began to harden. He should have waited and found out whether Metcalf was disposed to talk or to come at him with a chair leg, not rushed out before he knew. He felt a touch of disappointment in himself for having panicked, lost his bottle. He'd been in trickier situations before and stood his ground. Must be getting soft in his old age.

He even considered returning to the pub but that would have been compounding error upon error. Whatever Metcalf's original intentions, they weren't likely to have improved any by Harry's abrupt departure. He started walking again, away from the pub and towards where he'd parked his car.

To reach his afternoon's surveillance he had to drive back along Seven Sisters Road and thereby pass in front of the Three Musketeers. As he did so, a Ford Granada arrived from the opposite direction and stopped on the double yellow lines before the pub. Two men, both black, young and on the large side, got out of the car, swiftly crossed the pavement and went in through the door with that self-conscious, purposeful air of men on a mission.

Harry drove on, congratulating himself. What he'd put down to a failure of nerve suddenly looked a lot more like a triumph of good judgement.

His afternoon of surveillance was uneventful and allowed him to finish reading the novel. It also produced a single sighting of a visiting male for him to report to his client. What it meant for the client's marriage was then the client's own affair. Perhaps if Harry were to give him the novel as well it might help bring a sense of proportion to his wife's misdemeanours.

He made his customary last call at the office on his way home and was surprised to find Yvonne still there since it was after her usual time for leaving.

'Did you see your Mr Metcalf?' she asked.

Was that why she'd stayed on? To ask him about the one case she didn't really know anything about?

'Yes, I saw him.'

'Was he helpful?'

'Not a lot.'

'I was wondering why he should have been so difficult to trace. I suppose it's with him being a landlord. His phone-number and everything will be under the name of the pub and not his own.'

'I suppose so.'

'Anyway, you found him. That's the main thing.'

Not really, thought Harry. The main thing was that, having found him, he'd then managed to lose him again without sustaining grievous bodily harm.

'So you've now seen everybody on your list.'

'Yes.'

'Does that mean the case is closed?'

'I suppose it does, yes.'

'And will you be telling Mr Holliday that?'

'When I get round to it.'

He couldn't see any point to her questions. Though he noticed now that she was tense, excited even. Certainly not her usual phlegmatic self. And she had something more to say.

'Harry, I've got a confession to make.'

'What?'

'Promise you won't be angry with me.'

'I, er . . . yes, all right, I promise.'

What new surprise was she about to spring? More revelations about her unexpected love-life? Difficult to imagine why they might be expected to make him angry though. He waited.

'Something I've never told you about. Something that Mr Humphries had installed here in the office and that I forgot to mention when you took over and then . . . well, then it was too late.'

He looked around, puzzled. Something Clifford had installed . . .?

'You see, there were times, with some of our more sensitive cases, when he wanted his conversation with the client to be recorded. Without the client knowing of course.'

Harry's brain began to race. She knows about the Phil Holliday case, he thought. She's heard every word.

'So he had a sort of intercom installed between the

two offices. One-way. There's a microphone hidden in the wall next door in your office – I'll show you where it is – and then what I have here . . .' She opened a drawer of her desk. 'I've got a cassette-recorder that tapes whatever's said in your office. That is, when I switch it on.'

She looked at him, waiting nervously for his reaction.

'I see,' he said. 'Clever stuff.'

'And just for that first week I did put it on sometimes, just to, you know, check how you were getting along.'

'And how was I getting along?'

'Oh, very well.'

'And so you heard everything Phil Holliday told me?'

'Yes.'

And she visibly winced, every inch the plump, naughty school-girl waiting for the reprimand to descend.

But he didn't mind. Not really. He was amused by Clifford's deviousness and encouraged again in his opinion that Yvonne was a pretty smart operator and valuable ally. It also saved him the worry over whether or not to tell her about the Phil Holliday business since she already knew.

'Well, it's not just the intercom that's clever, then, is it?'

Seeing he wasn't annoyed, she gave a great sigh of relief and began to clean her glasses.

'I didn't know how to tell you. I thought you might have been furious. Now, I'll make us both a nice cup of tea, shall I?'

'Well, I don't know,' he said, looking at his watch. 'I thought I might call it a day. That's after you've shown me where this microphone is.'

But she hadn't taken any notice and was already fussing around with kettle and cups.

'I assume you didn't get anywhere with Frank

Metcalf this afternoon?'

'You can say that again.'

'And so what're you going to do now?'

'Not much I can do, is there?'

'Well, would you mind if we listened to the tape again?'

'What tape?'

'The tape of your conversation with Mr Holliday. I've still got it.'

And she put a cup of tea into his hands.

'Oh, have you?'

'Yes, I thought . . . well, I thought it might be useful.'

'I don't see how. All right, we can listen to it if you like. But I don't see that there's a lot of point.'

She hesitated. 'Well . . . I hope you won't think I'm trying to show off or anything . . . because I didn't realise it myself till I'd listened to the tape two or three times . . .'

'Realise what?'

'That there's something wrong with his story.'

Harry looked at her, baffled. 'What do you mean – wrong with it?'

'Well, shall we listen to it again? Only I don't want to tell you what I think in case it's me who's misunderstood. Why don't we listen to it again and see if you can spot it as well?'

Now intrigued, Harry said, 'OK. And do I get a prize if I get it right?'

But she was serious and eager and even locked the office door – 'Just so we're not disturbed' – before sitting behind her desk and opening the drawer in which the recorder was concealed.

'Ready?'

Harry nodded and she started the tape.

161

Here, says Les and reaches past me with the key we've done and sticks it in the panel and I give the button another dig and then we all start breathing again 'cause the doors are closing and we're on our way. Nobody says a word as we're going down. Les is still flexing his hand where he's been bitten and I notice that Vince is rubbing his shoulder and I wonder whether I got hit at all. We feel like we're in the slowest lift on earth and that every floor it's going to stop but it doesn't and we're finally there at the bottom and wondering what we're going to see when the doors open and praying it's not going to be a load of bobbies. Which it shouldn't be 'cause everything's going like clockwork. There's no bobbies, no anybody, only Neil waiting and by the looks of it he's done a good job. There's a clear passage to the doors that're standing open to the loading-bay. Nice and easy says Frank, no rush. Which is a laugh. All right? says Neil, and we tell him yes we are, and I wonder if we all look as terrified as he does. Probably not since we've been seeing action which lets you get it out of your system while he's just been standing there wondering what the hell's going on. We're pulling the trolley along, me and Frank, while the others are walking alongside sort of shielding it as best as they can. And suddenly you're glad it's a telly company you're nicking off 'cause all around there's all sorts of gear stacked and blokes lugging weird items about that I suppose they need for programmes like the Des O'Connor Show. So that nobody seems to be taking a lot of notice of us as we go out through the doors. Over here says Neil who's had time to see where the motors are parked with their drivers waiting inside 'em. They're squeezed in between two bloody great Fleet vans. The back of one of these vans is open and there are two blokes sitting there eating sandwiches. All right? says Ronnie and they nod and then carry on eating while we load the boxes into the cars. What about the trolley says Vince. Leave it says Frank. And the money's in and now all we have to do is get out through the barrier and still there's nothing happening from inside the building. You've left your trolley

162

says one of the blokes eating sandwiches. That's all right says Ronnie, you can have it. We get into the motors and drive to the barrier where we have to stop while another security bloke peers out at us from his little office.

XII

They heard the tape to its end and Yvonne switched off the recorder. His tea, untouched, had gone cold at his elbow and his arm had gone numb where he'd been resting it against the arm of the chair.

She was waiting for his reaction.

'Well,' he said, and cleared his throat. 'Yes.'

'You think I'm right? That there is something wrong?'

'I'm, er . . . I'm not sure.'

He had a suspicion of what she was getting at but didn't yet want to commit himself.

'Do you want to hear it again?'

'No,' he said. Then changed his mind. 'Well . . . perhaps parts of it. I wouldn't mind hearing parts of it again.'

'Right,' she said, and began to rewind the tape.

'But, look, this must be boring you to death. And it's gone six, you know that, do you?'

'Oh, that's all right. I'm in no hurry.'

He went and switched on the lights as dusk was already invading the office.

'Can I borrow this?' he said, taking a note-pad from her desk.

'Of course you can.'

He'd make some notes. Try and tie down some hard facts from out of the rambling account. It was all too easy to become mesmerised by the story and be carried along by it. He needed to remain detached. Make an objective assessment.

'Where do you want to start?'

He shrugged. 'Might as well be at the beginning.'

She started the tape. Harry heard his own voice again and pulled a little face. Did he always sound like that?

'No. Further on,' he instructed her. 'Where he starts talking about how the job was set up.'

She advanced the tape, stopping every few seconds to check where they'd reached so that they jumped their way through the preliminaries of Phil pleading with Harry to take the case and Harry saying no and then saying perhaps and then finally giving way.

Until they were at the first of the sections he wanted to hear.

First I hear of it is one night when I'm out pubbing it and I go in the King Billy that's down off Whitechapel Road and Les Pinfield's there and he says he knows this firm in North London that're doing a big job and do I want to come in on it? Course I'm very doubtful on account of I'm for the high-jump if I'm nicked again and who the hell is this firm anyway? But Les is very persistent and he says Ronnie Franks and Tommy Coyle are interested and I know they're good lads so I says well, go on then, what is it?

'OK,' said Harry, and Yvonne's finger came down, stopping the narration short. 'Now the bit where they meet up with the other firm.'

While Yvonne juggled with the controls to find the point he wanted, he took out a pen and made a list of names on his pad: 'PHIL HOLLIDAY, LES PIN-FIELD, RONNIE FRANKS, TOMMY COYLE'.

'Ready?'

'Yes.'

. . . And so a couple of days later Les takes us in his car to this flat that he says is Frank's, whoever Frank is. It's somewhere in Islington and there are these four blokes there, all strangers to me. Les does the introductions and it turns out

that Frank is Frank Metcalf and the other three are Neil Patterson, Vince Jardine and Maurice Scanlon. Which leaves me none the wiser but that's not necessarily a bad thing 'cause who wants to be famous in this game?

He stopped her there and added to the names on his list: 'FRANK METCALF, NEIL PATTERSON, VINCE JARDINE, MAURICE SCANLON'.

It reminded him of the identical list he'd first made and given Yvonne to chase up. They'd then been no more than names to him. Since when – with the unfortunate exceptions of Les Pinfield and Vince Jardine – they'd each one sprung to life. United for a brief period of time in their quest for half-a-million quid, they'd remained dispersed until now when Harry had arrived to pull the threads together again.

He agreed with Yvonne that there wasn't much point in hearing Phil spell out the plan for the robbery so they jumped ahead to where the preparations were beginning in earnest.

And the other main problem is getting us all inside the building and getting the motors where they have to be in the loading-bay. For which we need passes. Now Vince – the bloke that's been working in the place and whose original brainwave it is – he still has his pass that they've given him. And Les says he knows somebody reliable that can copy it. Great, says Frank, get 'em to make us a dozen then we'll have spares in case anybody loses one. And then one night, after it's gone dark, Vince takes Maurice Scanlon and they climb over into the car-park at the back of Fleet and nick a couple of parking-discs from two of the wagons that're out there.

Taking his note-pad, Harry wrote 'ORIGINAL PASS' next to 'VINCE JARDINE' and 'COPIES MADE' next to 'LES PINFIELD'. Then he wrote 'PARKING-DISCS' next to 'VINCE JARDINE' and 'MAURICE SCANLON'.

'What happens next?' he said, trying to remember.

'They get the keys made to operate the lift and let them into the store-room.'

She wound the tape forward, and there it was to prove her point.

There's a store-room that's near to the service-lift where we reckon we can bung the security guards and I go up one day with Ronnie and stand covering him while he checks out the lock so we can get ourselves a key for it. Something else we need a key for is the lift, one that'll over-ride all the buttons so that once we're in it with the money we can make sure it'll be bottom floor next stop and there won't be some berk stopping us on the second. So Ronnie goes in, all dressed up like a workman with a bag of tools, and he says to one of the security men, 'Scuse me, mate, do you have a key to immobilise this lift while I check out the alarm system? For you, anything, says the security man, and hands it over.

'KEYS' wrote Harry against the names of 'PHIL HOLLIDAY' and 'RONNIE FRANKS'.

'And then they have a sort of practice,' said Yvonne, 'where they just watch the money being delivered.'

'And that's when they decide they need to have somebody making sure their escape route's clear . . .?'

'Yes. It's here somewhere . . .'

And, becoming adept now at judging the speed of the tape, she found it for him.

There is just one problem though and it's Maurice that tells us about it. He's going to be driving one of the motors and he's been checking things out from the loading-bay end, making sure everything's clear for the getaway. Well, he tells us we'd never get that trolley out in a month of Sundays on account of there's all sorts of junk cluttering up the area that's between the lift and the doors where we want to come out. So there's some debate about this and it's agreed somebody'll have to be stationed down there to make sure we have a clear run from the lift to the loading-bay. Which nobody wants to do since it seems like a cop-out from the real business. In the end it's a choice between me and Neil Patterson and we cut a pack of cards and he draws a seven and as luck would have it I draw an eight.

Harry made a note against 'NEIL PATTERSON'.

Before going on, Yvonne said, 'We are thinking the same thing, aren't we?'

'I'm not sure what I'm thinking yet,' said Harry. 'Let's get on to when they're actually pulling the job.' Then something else occurred to him. 'Oh no. What about that emergency meeting they have the night before? What does he say about that again?'

Yvonne looked surprised. Clearly she couldn't see that it was of any importance. She'd already run the tape beyond that point and had to go back to find the relevant passage.

There's a last meeting at Frank's flat in Islington the night before we're due to go. Everybody's edgy 'cause suddenly you're thinking of everything that can go wrong and what'll happen if it does. And there's a lot of mistrust coming out — between the two firms, each wondering whether they can count on the other. Still they've got the motors, nicked from out in Oxford or somewhere.

'That'll do,' Harry interrupted. 'Doesn't have much to say about it, does he?'

'You think it's important?'

'Well, it's the one thing I couldn't get anybody to talk about. Not even Scanlon and he didn't seem to mind what he said about the rest of it. Anyway, never mind, let's get onto where they were doing it for real.'

Yvonne's fingers brought them forward to the day of the robbery itself.

I get up that morning feeling sick to my stomach and can't touch any breakfast.

'Further on,' said Harry. 'Where they start to meet up.'

Then by half-ten we meet up in the gents on the fourth floor.

'There?'
'Perfect.'
So she jumped it back and ran it again.

*Then by half-ten we meet up in the gents on the fourth
floor. At least them that're doing the heavy business do. The
drivers are doing their own thing making sure the cars are
parked nice and handy. And then of course there's Tommy in
the foyer with his bleeper. He's to give us three bleeps to tell us
the van's arrived, two to tell us they're in the building and one
that the lift's on its way. It must have looked like a queers'
convention in that fourth-floor bog. Les is already there when I
go in and then Vince and Frank arrive together. Every time
anybody comes in we have to be combing our hair or washing
our hands or having a pee – though you can only do so much of
that to order. Ronnie has us worried, not turning up till there's
only about five or ten minutes to the off and Frank in
particular is abusing him something rotten when all of a sudden
he comes in through the door all hot and bothered and telling us
about delays on the tube. But everybody shuts him up.*

'Great,' said Harry, raising his hand as a signal for her
to stop. 'Now just hang on a minute.' And he made
more notes on his pad, writing out a new list in which
the names appeared in a different order.

'Now what?' said Yvonne when he'd finished and
was looking thoughtfully at what he'd written. 'Do you
want to hear it all the way to the end from here?'

'What comes next?'

'Well, there's all that about the waiting and . . .'

'No, skip all that.' He felt more confident now of
what it was he was looking for. 'Can you find the
passage where the lift doors open and they have the
fight with the two guards?'

'That's a bit further on.'

She let the tape run and then there it was, as requested.

*So for a split second nobody moves. 'Cause we're looking at
the dolly-bird and she's looking at us and it gives her two
boy-friends in crash-hats time to put their act together and one*

169

*of 'em goes for the alarm button on the other side of the lift
while the other's fumbling with this truncheon he's got fastened
to his belt. And then Frank lets out a yell and the magic
moment's over and all hell's let loose. I manage to swing the
old iron bar and catch the bloke going for the alarm button
across his knuckles. Les grabs the bird and gets his hand over
her mouth while she's still taking a deep breath preparatory to
screaming her head off, and Ronnie, Vince and Frank come
piling past me to have a go at guard number two who's got his
truncheon off his belt at last but doesn't seem too sure what to
do with it. . . .*

This time Harry didn't write anything; just made a
mark against each name as it was mentioned.

'What next?'

'I'm not sure we need any more,' said Harry,
studying what he'd got on the pad.

'How about the end of the robbery when they're
escaping from the building?'

'You think I should?'

'Hard to say since you won't tell me what you're
thinking.'

She was enjoying herself immensely. It must have
been the nearest anyone in that office had ever got to
real detection with a puzzle to be solved and clues to be
collected along the way. He supposed he was enjoying it
himself, though beyond the entertainment of the
moment he couldn't help but be aware of the uncertain
mess in which he'd be left if things really were as he was
beginning to believe.

'Let's hear it, then.'

'I mean from where they come out of the lift to where
they get in the cars.'

Harry nodded.

*There's no bobbies, no anybody, only Neil waiting and by
the looks of it he's done a good job. There's a clear passage to
the doors that're standing open to the loading-bay. Nice and*

170

*easy says Frank, no rush. Which is a laugh. All right? says
Neil, and we tell him yes we are, and I wonder if we all look
as terrified as he does. Probably not since we've been seeing
action which lets you get it out of your system while he's just
been standing there wondering what the hell's going on. We're
pulling the trolley along, me and Frank, while the others are
walking alongside sort of shielding it as best they can. And
suddenly you're glad it's a telly company you're nicking off
'cause all around there's all sorts of gear stacked and blokes
lugging weird items about that I suppose they need for
programmes like the Des O'Connor Show. So that nobody
seems to be taking a lot of notice of us as we go out through the
doors. Over here says Neil who's had time to see where the
motors are parked with their drivers waiting inside 'em.*

And she stopped the tape.

Harry tossed his note-pad back onto the desk.

'Well . . .?' she asked.

'Yes.'

'Those eight names that're mentioned . . .?'

'There's one he keeps forgetting to mention. Five
doing the heavy stuff, one watching the lift doors, one
in the foyer, two driving . . . there were nine of the
buggers.'

171

I'm in the Jag with Les and Ronnie with Maurice driving and the Volvo's behind us with everybody else. What's he waiting for? says Ronnie, meaning the security bloke on the barrier. Which none of us knows. Here we are lined up in two motors with half-a-million quid and all waiting on this one berk to press a button. And then we see he's picked up a telephone. Oh Jesus, says Les. And we're all thinking the same – that they're on to us – and I look round at the Volvo wondering if we should rush the berk in the office when suddenly Maurice says Thank Christ and I see the barrier's going up. We pull out nice and slow and there's a break in the traffic so that we're away up Lisson Grove. We've done it, we've bloody done it we're all shouting and I realise I'm sweating like a pig and in need of a piss but that can wait 'cause all we need now is an even break and we're in the clear and I'll be pissing onto best china for the rest of my life. Take it easy we keep telling one another, we're not there yet. But we know that we are, or as near to it as you can get. We go down Sussex Gardens into Bayswater Road and only once do we really sweat and that's when we stop at some lights at Notting Hill and there's a cop car across the way facing. Don't look at 'em says Les. Which is easier said than done. Then the lights change and we cross on the junction, us going one way and the cops the other and after that I think well that has to be it, we must have done it now. We do the switch-over at Holland Park, the idea being that when the cops do eventually find the motors they'll think we're heading west. Then we all cram into the Volkswagen, not forgetting the money since it would have been a shade unfortunate at that stage to have left it in the boot. And we head back north. And now everybody's talking telling one another what they thought when the berk wouldn't put his barrier up and when we stopped at the lights and saw the cop car. Till finally we're in Kentish Town and Neil's directing us to this warehouse he's got which is under some railway arches. And it's ideal 'cause we can drive right in and close the doors and there's no windows. No bogs either so we have to

take it in turns to slip outside and piss up against the wall. You
might have laid on some coffee, says Ronnie, only joking but
Neil says, Oh might I, and produces two flasks of it which is
much appreciated. And then Frank tells us all to shut up and
that we haven't finished yet. He reminds us that if we're
nicked now there isn't a brief on God's earth could get us off
with less than ten years apiece. So we all calm down again and
there isn't much more said even when we knock the tops off the
boxes and see all the money there, stacks of it, more than we
could ever have counted except that the bank have made it easy
for us and put most of it in wrappers that say five hundred or a
thousand on 'em. So we clear a space on the floor and make
piles of it, each pile being ten thousand. And it comes to
fifty-seven piles and some over. Then we have to divide it,
which everybody works out different till Neil produces a
calculator to stop the disputes. It's agreed that you go as soon as
you've got your wack. That way we're leaving at different
times and not all marching out together, all carrying Tesco
carrier-bags stuffed with tenners. Maurice goes first, then
Vince, then Ronnie, and I'm fourth. I shake hands with
everybody and then get the tube home. I manage to get back
while Margie's still collecting the eldest from school which
means I can stick the loot in a hole I've already dug in the
garden. Then I fill the hole in and persuade the dog to crap on
top of it as camouflage. After that the hardest part is just
leaving it there. Till the hue-and-cry dies down and then about
a month later I tell Margie what I've done. And after she's
gone bonkers and had a shout and a cry I get her to believe this
really is the last time and I show her the advert in the paper for
this newsagent's business I'm thinking of going for.

XIII

Next morning he went to see Phil Holliday at his shop. As he went in, he noticed the West Ham sticker in the corner of the window. Phil was serving school-kids with sweets and so Harry had to wait. The shop must be a small goldmine, he thought, what with morning and evening deliveries and counter business as well, a better investment than Fleet would have ever found for their money.

Then Phil was free and they went into the back.

'You've found out anything?' asked Phil, anxious and hopeful.

'I think I have, yes.'

'You know who's sending the letters?'

'I know who it might be.'

'Who?'

'Ah well, see, that's the problem. I don't know his name.'

'He wasn't one of us that did the job, then?'

'Oh yes, he was that all right.'

'Well, I've given you all the names,' said Phil, puzzled.

'You're sure about that?'

'Certainly. There was me, Les, Ronnie, Tommy, Neil, Vince, Maurice and Frank.'

'And the other one,' said Harry. 'What about the other one?'

Phil looked at him. 'Other one . . .?'

'Number nine.'

Phil shook his head as if to say he didn't know what Harry was talking about. But Harry, who knew all too well, wasn't going to let him act his way out of this one.

'Don't try and let on you don't know. 'Cause you know all right, and you've known all along.' He resisted a strong inclination to grab the other man by the throat and bounce his head against the wall. After all, this was a client: he might as well pay through the nose as bleed through it. 'I've risked my neck for you. I've been asking some very unhealthy questions on your behalf because you came to me begging for help. And now what do I find? That you've been playing clever buggers all along, telling me there was eight of you on this job when all the time there was nine!'

Phil cleared his throat and then gave a small shrug and only finally said, 'All right. There was, yes.'

Harry should have belted him. He should have belted him for messing him around and for placing him in jeopardy and because it would have been nice to have belted somebody just at that moment.

But he didn't. He just took a deep breath and a kick at a pile of newspapers.

'Who was he, then, number nine?'

'His name was Alex Stone.'

It left Harry none the wiser.

'And what's special about him that nobody thinks to tell me about him?' And then, before Phil could answer: 'And I want it all now. You know what I mean? I've been pissed around on this for long enough so I want every last bit of it and if I have the slightest impression for one moment that I'm not getting it then I'm going to get very angry, and I do mean very angry. Understood?'

'Yes.'

'It'd better be.'

Phil went to the door, checked there was no-one listening outside, then closed it again.

'This is just between you and me, right?'

'Who's Alex Stone?' said Harry.

'Somebody Les knew. Somebody he knew from some club or other up in town.'

'And?'

'And he, er . . . well, he found out what we was up to.'

'Les told him?'

'Must have, yes. Though, course, Les wouldn't have it. But he was Les's mate. So it was down to Les as far as the rest of us was concerned.'

'Go on.'

'Well, the first we hears about him was just three or fours days before we're due for the off. The word goes round there's this feller that's rumbled us and that wants in. Course we said no chance but then Les gets very worried and says well look, if we don't want him in then he's going to go shouting his mouth off and then there's no way we're ever going to come out the other end of this as free men.'

'He knew all about the job, then, did he, this Alex Stone?'

Phil nodded. 'Seemed like it.'

'That can't have improved Les's popularity. Or his life-expectancy I wouldn't have thought.'

Phil agreed. 'Frank went for him and there was a bit of a barney but everybody pulled 'em apart 'cause we was so close by that stage – I mean it was like we could almost reach out and touch the money – so there was nobody wanted to upset anything.'

'I can imagine. So what did you do?'

'Well finally two of 'em – that was Neil and Ronnie I think – they went along with Les to meet this Alex. To see if they might not be able to pay him off or else

176

perhaps lean on him a little and put the frighteners on him.'

'Didn't work?'

'No chance. He was a real nutter, real hard-case. He wanted in and that was the end of it. So then we did some quick asking around, see if anybody had heard of him, and the word that came back was that his own mother wouldn't turn her back on him. So either we had to call the job off or else have him in on it.'

'Or else have him taken care of.'

'Well, yes.'

'And this was why you had the meeting the night before the off.'

'Yes.'

'Was he there?'

'He was there for part of it.'

'And you told him he was in.'

'Yes. And a lot of other things besides, like what would happen to him if he opened his mouth. He was going to be one of the drivers. Driving the Volvo. I mean it wasn't that we couldn't use him 'cause we was a bit stretched on the job as it was with just the eight of us. And there was still enough dough to go round. The trouble with Alex coming in, it was just that, well . . .'

'You didn't trust him.'

'No. Never would do neither. Which was why we had the second part of the meeting. The part where he wasn't there.'

'And what was that all about?'

'What to do with him afterwards.'

'And what did you decide?'

'That Les was going to have to deal with him.'

'Just Les?'

'Yes. Well, it was Les's fault. Les's responsibility. And, see, it had to be one of us doing it on his tod 'cause we'd all sworn not to meet again afterwards.'

'And how did Les feel about that?'

'Not very happy, but then he hadn't got much choice. If he hadn't have agreed to it then Frank and one or two of the others would have done for him.'

Harry nodded. He'd met Frank and could understand how Les must have been feeling.

'When you say that Les was going to have to deal with this Alex Stone . . .'

'Yes?'

'You mean kill him?'

Phil shrugged. 'Either kill him himself or have somebody else do it for him, yes.'

'But not till after the robbery.'

'No. 'Cause, see, it was too near. We didn't want anything to happen that might have alerted the coppers, anything that might have got in the way of the job.'

'And did Les agree to all this?'

'He didn't have no choice. Only he wasn't to do anything till after we'd shared out the money and split. Then, however he set about it, it wasn't going to be anything to do with the rest of us.'

'And did he kill him?'

Phil hesitated a moment, then said, 'Yes.'

'You're sure?'

'Well, I never saw the body nor nothing. But what I did see . . . well, the idea was for Les to put an advert in the *Evening Standard* once the job was done.'

'An advert?'

'In the personal column, yes. Sounds a bit silly now but anyway what it had to say was – If one green bottle should accidentally fall, there'll be eight green bottles standing on the wall.'

'And the advert appeared?'

Phil nodded. 'A week after the job. And nobody's ever heard a word about Alex Stone from that day to this so . . . well, I reckon Les must have done it like he said he would.'

Harry said nothing for a moment but tried to sort out his thoughts. If Les Pinfield had indeed carried out his allotted task of murder then Alex Stone could hardly have been himself in the business of murder and blackmail some eight years later. And if Les Pinfield had done no more than place the advert in the *Standard* and keep his fingers crossed, what then had happened to the dangerous Mr Stone? Why had he remained out of sight for so long before abruptly resurfacing to demand money with menaces?

Phil mistook his silence for doubt and said nervously, 'It's the truth, Harry boy. Every word of it.'

Harry didn't doubt that. It wasn't only Phil's frightened manner but the way the jigsaw had now come together, revealing the secrets of the last-minute meeting.

'What about the money though?'

'How's that?'

'After the robbery. Did this Alex Stone walk off with his share of the half-million or what?'

'Yes. Well, he had to. There was no other way.'

'Fifty-odd thousand quid? And nobody minded kissing goodbye to it?'

'Well, we minded all right, yes. But under the circumstances . . . And I mean it was only, what, seven or eight thousand each. Which when you've got fifty thousand coming anyway doesn't seem all that much.'

'I suppose not. But then if Alex Stone wasn't going to live long enough to spend it . . .?'

'Yes, well, there was a lot of talk about that. But in the end what we reckoned was that there was nothing we could do about it. No way we could share it, not without us all coming together again, which we didn't want. And if Les could get his hands on it, well then good luck to him 'cause he'd probably need the extra anyway if he was to pay to have Stone done away with.'

'You think that's what happened? That Les Pinfield

paid somebody else to kill Stone?'

'More than likely. I mean Les wasn't a killer. It wasn't his sort of thing at all. But he did know a lot of people and could probably have fixed it. Certainly if he had Alex's share of the loot to play with as well as his own.'

'You never asked him about it?'

'No.'

'Why not?'

'Oh, come on, Harry boy. There are some things you're better off not knowing. And by the time I saw old Les again it was like months later and I was setting up here in business and all that was well behind me, which was where I wanted to leave it.'

It all made sense. Les Pinfield had paid to have Alex Stone quietly bumped off, gambling that he'd then manage to get his hands on Stone's share of the takings and come out showing a profit. Its drawback as a solution was that it ruled out the possibility of any link between Alex Stone and Les Pinfield's own death or between Alex Stone and the blackmail letters received by Les Pinfield and Phil Holliday. Was it, then, simply coincidence that, eight years ago, Les Pinfield had talked too much and almost sabotaged the entire operation and had now been the first to receive a blackmail letter and then a knife in the guts for failing to respond to it?

Some people were just plain unlucky. Either Les Pinfield was one, or else there was a connection between the two events which Harry had yet to discover.

'Tell me about Alex Stone.'

'What is there to tell? I only saw him two or three times. Which was more than enough.'

'How old was he?'

''Bout thirty.'

'And Les knew him from where?'

'Don't know exactly. Clubs. Places up in town.'

'Where did he live?'

'Not a clue.'

It wasn't exactly adding up to a detailed dossier. Even the question of whether he was alive or dead remained in doubt.

'Oh, one thing I do remember about him though,' said Phil.

'What?'

'He was Australian. Spoke with an Australian accent.'

Which was a start. Though it wouldn't have made him the only Aussie villain resident in London, not by a long chalk.

'And more than that I can't tell you, Harry. Honest to God I can't.'

'Have you heard any more on the blackmail side of things?'

'No.'

'Well, maybe we've scared him off then, eh. Whoever he is.'

'But do you think it might be Alex?' asked Phil. 'That he might still be alive and it's him?'

Harry shrugged. The only people who might have answered that were Les Pinfield, who was dead, and Alex Stone, rumoured to be in a similar condition. All that was certain was that they couldn't have killed each other.

At least now he could discuss the case with Yvonne. She sat eating a carton of chicken chow mein while he summarised all that Phil Holliday had told him. The aroma of Chinese cooking contrasted sharply with the carbon-tetrachloride from downstairs.

'So that really doesn't get you any further,' she said between mouthfuls.

'No.'

'Except that they're not only robbers, they're also conspirators to murder.' She seemed to relish the thought.

'That's if Alex Stone was ever actually killed.'

181

'You don't think he was?'

Harry hesitated. Since talking to Phil Holliday, there'd been an idea growing at the back of his mind. It was the fact of Stone's being Australian that had seeded it there.

'You think he's still alive?' she urged.

'Well . . . suppose you were Les Pinfield.'

'Yes?'

'And you've landed yourself in a lot of bother because you've got drunk or whatever and you've gone and let on to this mate of yours about this big robbery that you're involved in. Only then this mate of yours starts insisting he wants in on it. Failing which he's going to blow the whistle on the whole thing.'

'I wouldn't be very happy,' said Yvonne, folding up the take-away foil container and dropping it in the waste-paper basket.

'No. Because you're frightened the other seven blokes you're in with are going to chop you up into little pieces. And the only way you persuade 'em not to is that you promise you'll take care of Mr Stone once the job is over and done with.'

'You mean I promise that I'll kill him?'

'Yes.'

'Aren't I awful.' And she went to fill the kettle. 'D'you want a cup of tea?'

'Yes please. So anyway the job's done and now you've got to keep your promise.'

'Or find a way out of it.'

Harry chuckled. 'Just what I was thinking. And I mean I know I've never met Les Pinfield – never will – but I wouldn't think he was all that different from any of the others.'

Not that those other six, varying as they did from the amiable to the paranoid, had had much in common. Excepting only that none of them seemed much

182

concerned as to what had become of the others.

'Meaning what?'

'Meaning he'll have done whatever would be best for Les Pinfield. I mean they all go on about how well they all worked together, but my main impression is that, once it was over, they just didn't want to know.'

'No honour among thieves.'

'Not a lot, no.'

Something Harry knew more about than most. He'd been in the Jack O'Lantern the night Nobby Reilly and Felix James had got drunk together and sung 'Auld Lang Syne' with their arms around each other's shoulders; a week later James had been axed to death by Stan 'The Clown' Phibbs who was Reilly's henchman.

'So what do you think Les Pinfield would have done, then?'

'Well, he'd have to get Alex Stone to disappear. Otherwise he'd be in bother himself.'

'Yes.'

'Now, Stone was Australian. In fact, that's about the only thing Phil Holliday seems able to remember about him. So what I'm wondering is whether Les Pinfield persuaded him to go back there.'

'And how would he do that?'

'By telling him the truth. Or near enough. That the others were out to kill him. Not mentioning, of course, that he was the one supposed to do it. Just warning Stone that he had to get out of the country as quick as he could.'

'And then he put the advert in the newspaper.'

'Exactly.'

'I think you're probably right,' said Yvonne, and gave him his cup of tea.

He now thought he was, too. But then that still raised a whole batch of other questions. If Stone had fled back to Australia eight years ago, why had he now chosen to return? Had he run out of funds and seen the prospect of blackmailing the other members of the gang as an easy way of getting some? But then why start on Les Pinfield, his one-time friend and his only ally? Had he simply been the only one he could locate?

However, this was speculation running wild. Essential first to prove whether Alex Stone were alive or dead.

'I know what you're going to ask,' said Yvonne as he opened his mouth to speak. 'And the answer's I don't know but we can try.'

'What, try and find out whether Alex Stone ever did go back to Australia?'

'Yes. The Australian police, British Immigration . . . if he has been alive for the past eight years then somebody must have caught sight of him somewhere.'

It later occurred to Harry that he had a possible lead of his own, though one that depended more on the British villains' old boys' network than on the Australian police computer. He'd once worked as bouncer in an Earls Court disco where even the DJs had been Aussies. It had since closed and re-opened several times under new names though always under the same old management – a gentleman by the name of Graham Bonnington-Price, who had operated in Earls Court for so long he knew more about the comings and goings of expat Aussies than did the Australian High Commission. It was worth a phone-call.

He found the number. The voice that answered had an Australian accent: it reassured Harry that the place hadn't changed.

'Yeah?'

'Is Mr Bonnington-Price there?'

'No.'

'Do you know when he will be?'

184

'No.'

'Well, look, if he's got a minute could he give me a ring? It's Harry Sommers here.'

A pause, then: 'I'll tell him.'

'It's the Coronet Private Investigation Agency.' And he gave the number.

There was another pause and Harry was about to hang up when the voice at the other end said, 'What's it about?'

Resisting the temptation to give any one of several rude answers that sprang to mind, Harry said, 'It's a case I'm working on. I'm trying to trace somebody.'

The phone at the other end was replaced.

Up yours too, cobber, thought Harry.

He wasn't really expecting any more enthusiastic a reception at his next port of call, which was 48 Ashley Road, Chiswick.

He was going to return the book, the American novel she'd lent him and that he'd at last finished reading. He could, of course, have posted it; or simply kept it. But he was pursuing a missing person enquiry that took him into West London and, more importantly, it irked him to leave things as they were without a last face-to-face meeting with Miss Jill Hanscombe. They'd parted ungraciously, via the telephone, leaving him with what he couldn't help but feel was an unduly large share of the blame for the unfortunate duffing-up of her ex-husband. If she wanted to set straight the record between them, then this would give her the opportunity. If she didn't, then at least she'd have her book back.

It was mid-evening when he arrived. The purple Mini was parked along the road. So far, so good. If she had company he'd just give her the book and go.

He pressed the third bell down, there was a pause and then she answered, still as hesitant and defensive-sounding as ever. Perhaps her ex was still sniffing around.

'Yes?'

'It's Harry Sommers. I've brought your book back.'

She gave a little 'Oh' of surprise and then the buzzer went, he pushed on the front door and was inside.

She didn't mind seeing him, then. Or had she pressed the door-release instinctively and was she now regretting it?

He hoped she wasn't. Going up the carpeted stairs, he suddenly knew that what he wanted more than anything was for them to get it back together again.

She opened the door as he approached. She looked as she'd done before when he'd seen her after school, a bit careworn, as though some of the gloss had been rubbed off. Good, he thought, there's nobody with her.

'Well, hello,' she said.

It was neutral. Begged the question. Had he come as friend or foe?

'Hello. I brought the book.'

He held it out and she took it. It felt an absurd gesture, a childish excuse for his being there and one which neither of them believed.

'Thanks. Do you want to come in?'

He stepped forward but, instead of passing her, put his arms around her and pulled her to him. He caught a glimpse of her face, like that of a startled rabbit, and then he kissed her.

'Well,' she said, when he finally let her go and stepped into the flat, 'and I thought you'd come to give me my book back.'

'Then you're not as clever as you're supposed to be,' he said, as surprised by his impulsive action as she'd been.

'Am I not?'

'No. Even I didn't think it was much of an excuse. I

just couldn't think of anything better.'

She smiled – thank God – and said, 'Well, sit down. How are you?'

'Not so bad. And how're you?'

'Oh, fine, yes.'

'Still teaching?'

'Yes. Are you still . . . detecting?'

'Most of the time.'

She offered him a drink but by this time the devil-may-care mood that had suddenly gripped him and caused him to kiss her had begun to ebb and he muttered something about intruding but she said no, of course he wasn't, and so he said well, all right then, yes. She brought an already-opened bottle of wine.

'About your husband,' he said.

She continued with the wine-pouring and said nothing.

'Does he still hang around checking the cars outside your door or has he found himself a different hobby?'

'I haven't heard from him,' she said carefully, 'since the night you . . . you came into contact with him.'

'Good. Because you know he got everything he asked for. That was a very silly game to be playing at his age.'

'He can be a very silly man.'

'Can he?'

'Sometimes.'

'Well then, I'll tell you something.' She looked at him. 'I think you're even sillier. Letting a mix-up like that spoil things for us.'

There was a long pause. Short of leaving, Harry could think of no way of ending it and so sat toying with his glass of wine.

'Perhaps you're right,' she said finally.

'I'm sure I am.'

'I didn't think you'd want to see me again. Not after seeing what sort of mess my life was in.'

He gave a little laugh and shook his head.

'Anyway, cheers,' she said, raising her glass.

'Cheers.'

'And what did you think of the book?'

'Oh, it's, er . . . yes, it's good. Yes.'

She waited, then said, 'That it?'

'Yes.'

There was another pause. She asked him if he'd had any good cases lately and he told her about a couple – though not about Phil Holliday. He asked her about Jade Grodzinski. She said her work was as bad as ever but her teeth were improving and she'd had the brace removed. After which he invited her to tell him about her marriage.

Her husband, she said, was someone she'd met at university, then lost track of, then bumped into again when they'd each separately established themselves in London, she as a teacher, he as a news reporter. Why they'd ever married she couldn't remember but it'd been an intense and acrimonious relationship that had led him to drink and her to a (not very serious) attempt at suicide. She'd sought help through psychiatry and he through an affair with an older woman. Both of which seemed about equally ineffectual. Then came the first of several moments of violence between them when he would attack her, then, in a fit of remorse, drink himself into insensibility.

At which point things really began to go downhill.

All this and a great deal more took the evening to tell. When Harry's stomach began to rumble they both admitted they hadn't eaten and went out to a trattoria two blocks away. They came back hand in hand and, since it seemed the natural as well as the highly desirable thing to do, retired to bed for the remainder of the story.

It was the early hours by the time he tiptoed away down the stairs, taking with him the scent of her body and her promise to ring him tomorrow. She had even joked: 'Say hello to my husband if he's out there.' But he wasn't. There was only a youthful policeman passing on his beat. Before he could stop himself, Harry had given him a beaming smile and received a rather guarded one in return.

He felt light-headed with delight at the evening's outcome and in no mood for hurrying homeward. Finding himself in Kensington and doubting that his phone-call of the afternoon would ever bear fruit, he decided on a small detour to Earls Court. Call in for a glass of lager and hope there might be some information to go with it.

The disco/night club that he'd known and guarded as Delilah's had been rechristened the Golden Temple but didn't otherwise look to have changed much.

There was a sharp-looking dolly-bird on the door and, beside her, a square man in a dinner jacket who stood with his arms folded across his chest and looked Harry up and down as he approached. Harry gave them both a smile; neither smiled back.

'You a member?' asked the dolly-bird.

'No. Is Mr Bonnington-Price around?'

The dolly-bird glanced at her dinner-jacketed companion.

'I'm an old mate of his,' said Harry.

'What's your name?'

'Harry Sommers.'

The man went to a wall-phone and began to speak into it.

'Nice night,' beamed Harry at the dolly-bird.

'Not if you've been stood here as long as I bleeding have.'

The man returned.

'He says you're to go through. You know where his office is, do you?'

Graham Bonnington-Price was an entrepreneur, a lover of clubland, an old Etonian whose family had fallen on hard times. That is, been rumbled by the fraud squad. He now didn't own much of anything himself but was the front man for those who did.

He greeted Harry like a long-lost brother, made him sit down and recount what had happened to him since they'd last met. The idea of the detective agency pleased him enormously.

'Wonderful, Harry. Private eye. It suits you. It really does.'

'Actually I've got to be honest,' said Harry.

'Not here you don't.'

'I mean it's not just a social call. I am actually looking for somebody and was wondering if you'd heard a whisper or anything.'

'Go on. Try me.'

'He's Australian.'

'Shortens the odds.'

'Name's Alex Stone.'

Graham Bonnington-Price stared at him in astonishment.

'What's the matter?' said Harry.

'Alex . . .?'

'You know him?'

'I not only know him – he works here!'

It was Harry's turn for the astonished stare.

'You're serious?'

'Of course I am. He's only been with us a few weeks, mind. Helping out behind the bar.'

'Is he here tonight?'

'Well, funny you should ask that. Because he should have been. Only he hasn't turned up.'

An idea struck Harry. It wasn't a pleasant one and he

190

hesitated to have it confirmed.

'Was he here this afternoon?'

'I think he might have been. Hang on.' He fumbled around among sheets of paper and came up with some kind of rota. 'Here it is. Yes, he was down for this afternoon. And he was in. Because I remember someone saying it was odd he'd gone off for what should have been a couple of hours' break but then never returned.'

Harry gave a groan of dismay. For once he'd hit the bull's-eye without knowing it, and succeeded only in turning himself into the target.

'Nothing the matter, is there?'

'I rang here this afternoon. Asking if you was in. And some bloke answered but he didn't give his name or anything. Now could that have been Alex Stone?'

'What, you rang the club number? The one in the book?'

'Yes.'

'Then yes, that'd be Alex all right. You'd have gone through to the bar and he would have answered. Bit of luck for you, eh? There you are looking for him and you end up talking to him without knowing it.'

XIV

Could he really have said enough to have alerted Stone, in their brief phone conversation, to the fact it was Stone himself he was after? Just what had he said?

Well, firstly, he'd asked to speak to Mr Bonnington-Price. Then he'd identified himself as Harry Sommers of the Coronet Private Investigation Agency. And then he'd said he was trying to trace someone.

Not much, but probably enough for Mr Stone to be able to fill in the blanks for himself.

They had, of course, spoken by phone before. Or so Harry now had to suppose. Shortly after he'd visited Ronnie Franks and Neil Patterson, in the early days of the case, there had come the threatening phone-call, warning him to lay off. Too long ago now to remember if the caller had an accent but, assuming it had been Stone, it meant he'd been aware of Harry's investigations all along. On top of which he'd now been tipped off – by Harry himself – that these investigations had led him to look for someone amid the antipodean night-life of Earls Court.

It didn't take a genius to add that lot together and come up with the answer that Harry Sommers had you fingered for Les Pinfield's murder and was coming looking for you. And it didn't take a psychopath to decide that your best bet was to find Harry Sommers before he found you.

Find him and kill him.

★   ★   ★

London was enjoying an Indian summer, a temporary respite from the winds of autumn before winter established its grip. Commuters went back into summer clothing and the heating was switched off in public buildings.

For his part, Harry went back to the kind of watchfulness he hadn't needed to display since the gangland rivalries that had raged about his head some ten years earlier when his role of minder for one establishment or another had put him in the firing-line. It wasn't a matter of carrying arms. He'd only once been given a gun, which he'd worn rather self-consciously for a day or two, then politely returned. Knives had never been his scene either. He'd rely now, as he always had, on his well-educated fists which had ensured his survival thus far.

His greatest problem was that Stone could find him whenever he chose and so held the initiative. Harry could only wait and remain watchful.

Still, he wasn't going to become paranoid about it, cowering indoors and wearing bullet-proof vests. Not, anyway, in this weather. It would be business as usual – surveillance, process-serving, missing person enquiries – though he would, in military terms, be in a condition of general alert. Which, translated into non-military terms, meant he was making sure he'd have the chance to do for Stone before Stone did for him.

None of which was going to interfere with his born-again relationship with Jill. She rang him as promised.

'Hello, it's me.'

'Great. How are you?'

'Very well, believe it or not. What are you doing this morning?'

'Serving a county court summons on a shoe shop.'

'Why? What have they ever done to you?'

'Nothing. Never put a foot wrong.'

She laughed. 'I have to teach Keats to the sixth form. Couldn't we do a swap?'

'Why don't I meet you tonight to talk about that?'

She said she had a meeting tonight and so it was to be the following night. He trekked across London and they went to the trattoria two blocks away. Only by then her mood seemed to have dipped and flattened.

'Look, Harry . . .'

'What?'

'Do you think this is wise?'

'Do I think what is wise?'

'Us.'

'I think it's marvellous. I couldn't give a damn about whether it's wise or not.'

She sighed. 'I just think you're going to find me rather hard work, that's all.'

'Too late.'

'What?'

'I already have found you hard work.'

'Exactly.'

'It's what I like most about you.'

The smile this drew from her was one she did her best to conceal. It was as though she wanted him to know she wouldn't easily be made happy. She'd lived too long and been through too much to believe that being swept off your feet could lead to anything but a sharp fall on to your backside.

Harry had at first put this down to her being a classy bird; they were, he supposed, all moody to one degree or another. Only later had he decided it was more to do with her own personality and past. Nor was he any longer so intimidated as to let her get away with it. Their session in bed had redefined their relationship: he was now going to deal with her sudden fits of gloom by refusing to recognise them.

194

'Anyway I've been out with more miserable birds than you.'

'I'm glad to hear it.'

'Yeah, you're a bundle of laughs compared to some of 'em.'

Her face slipped into a smile.

'I don't believe it.'

But she took his hand and gave it a squeeze, so he thought, well, he couldn't be doing too badly, considering what a complicated lady she was.

'Hey . . .!'

The cry came from a man flying backwards into a shop window.

There was a thud as he met the glass and Harry, who'd flung him against it, waited for the smash. But it never came. The window shook but stayed intact. The man, more shaken than the window, gaped at Harry.

'What the hell . . .?'

'Sorry, mate,' said Harry, realising now it'd been a false alarm.

He'd been walking to the office, past a row of shops, and had to side-step two women, a manoeuvre that'd brought him into sudden, hard contact with a man in leather jacket and jeans coming the opposite way. Geared up to expect sudden attack, his reaction had been instinctive and immediate. He'd sent the man slamming against the shop window. And only then, too late, seen his empty hands and the look of outrage and alarm on his face.

'I am sorry,' he repeated. 'Look, are you all right?'

The man evidently was. Realising he wasn't going to be further attacked, his alarm disappeared and outrage took over.

'What the hell do you think you're playing at?'

'It was a misunderstanding.'

195

'Are you some kind of maniac or something?'

Harry could only keep on apologising. A few passers-by had stopped to watch and the shop-owner came out to examine his window, demanding to know what was going on.

'He bleeding well threw me into it!'

'Sorry,' said Harry. 'Don't know what came over me.'

'You want locking up.'

Until, in the end, all he could do was walk away, leaving the small commotion behind him.

'Got it,' said Yvonne as he walked into the office.

'Got what?'

'The information from Australia. Or rather our friendly policeman got it for us and we paid him for it. Listen to this.' And she read from her notes. 'Alexander John Stone, born Melbourne, 4th August 1952. Educated Hill Crest High School . . .' She broke off from reading and looked up at him. 'Then he's got a police record as long as your arm. Do you want to hear it?'

'I'll have a look at it later. Does it tell us whether he's still alive or not?'

'Yes.'

'Yes, it does? Or yes, he is?'

'Yes, he is. Or at least he was six months ago.'

'How do they know that?'

'Because six months ago – 17th May to be precise – was the date of his release from prison.'

'He'd been in the nick . . .?'

'Yes.' As always, she was enjoying surprising him with the information she'd produced, displaying it as though it were a rabbit pulled from an empty hat. 'An Australian nick.'

'And how long had he been in for?'

'How long do you think?'

'I don't know.'

196

'Well, you were wondering where he'd disappeared to after doing the robbery . . .'

'Oh, I see. You mean he's been in the nick since then?'

'More or less. He served seven years. So, allowing for a few months on either side, that would explain why Mr Stone hasn't been seen around much since he worked with your friend Mr Holliday.'

'And what was he in for, do we know?'

'Conspiracy and assault. And it wasn't his first offence either.'

She passed Harry her notes. They detailed a career of juvenile and then adult crime in which 'assault' and 'carrying weapons' figured prominently. As a character-reference, it would have recommended Alex Stone only to the Mafia, and then even they might have had reservations. As far as Harry was concerned, it confirmed everything Phil Holliday's account had suggested: the man in pursuit of him was vicious and extremely dangerous.

'He sounds like the sort of person you're better off keeping well away from,' observed Yvonne.

'You can say that again.'

He hadn't told her of his phone-call to the Golden Temple and the way he'd unwittingly alerted Stone to his interest in him. Nor did he see any point in telling her now. She'd only be alarmed; might even insist they inform the police and then who could say where things would end? Possibly with Phil Holliday and colleagues behind bars and so many people out for Harry's blood he'd have to emigrate himself.

'So what are you going to do?' she asked.

'Not much I can do, is there?'

'That's what I was thinking. I mean Mr Holliday wanted us to find who'd sent him the blackmail letter. Well, we've as good as done that. I mean assuming it was this Alexander Stone.'

'Yes.'

'So the case is closed, is it?'

She wanted him to agree, to get the Agency out of the whole sticky and dangerous mess.

'I suppose it is.'

'So shall I make up Mr Holliday's account?'

Harry hesitated. They could give Phil Holliday his account all right, but the case wouldn't be closed, either for him or for Phil, until Alex Stone had been flushed from the shadows.

'You can make it up,' said Harry, 'but don't send it yet. Let's just hang onto it for another day or two. Just to be on the safe side.'

'And so how're you tonight, then?' he asked Jill, arriving to collect her on the Friday evening.

She thought about it, then gave her considered opinion.

'Quite good.'

'I don't believe it,' he said in mock surprise. 'What is it, the end of the week? No more teaching for two days?'

'Don't ask me to think about it. I might decide I've got it wrong and should be depressed.'

'Must be my influence.'

'No, you're right. It's because it's the weekend and I've no more teaching for two days.'

They went out for a meal and he told her about the latest developments in the Phil Holliday case, though soft-pedalling on the precariousness of his own situation.

'So what can you do?'

'Oh, not a lot. Just try and keep clear of cases like this in future.'

'You make it sound normal, the way they carried out a robbery and got away with it.'

198

'It is normal for some people.'

'Which people?'

'Villains. Though there aren't many manage to make much of a living out of it. I mean for all the villains that start out, most of 'em end up dead or in the nick or . . .' – he couldn't resist it – '. . . running private detective agencies.'

She gave him a glance but let it pass.

'Is there really much of an underworld?'

'Not organised, no. Just a few characters who're King Rat in their own particular district.'

'And what're they like, these people?'

So he entertained her with stories, abridged here and there, of exploits he'd witnessed or heard of. Like most people born to be forever on the right side of the law, she was curious about those who weren't. Perhaps that was part of his attraction for her. Part of hers for him had been that she came from the other side of the tracks; it had to work the other way round too.

'You don't mix with these people any more, do you?' she asked when they came back to the flat.

'Why?' he said teasingly. 'What would you do if I said I was in on a bank job next week?'

'Well, I don't think I'd make a very good gangster's moll.'

'You don't know till you've tried.'

'Oh yes, I do,' she said, suddenly emphatic.

He took the implied warning and left it at that. A reformed villain she could just about take; a practising one would find himself out with the empties. He even wondered whether he'd been wise to talk so openly, lest learning about his former associates might cause her second thoughts about associating with him.

Till she removed all such fears by suddenly asking, 'Do you have to go tonight?'

'No.'

'Then don't.'

So that he was still there the following morning, awakening before she did and knowing immediately where he was but less sure just what it was he must have done in his past life that'd been so good as to land him there.

They had breakfast and did some shopping. Then they set off on a long walk that brought them across Hyde Park and ended in Trafalgar Square where Harry insisted they went in the National Gallery.

'And what about this?' he asked at each picture they came to.

'I don't want to lecture you, Harry,' she protested. 'For God's sake, don't turn me into your teacher.'

'But I want to know.'

'Then buy a guide-book.'

He did so and insisted on reading aloud what it said on each picture. After an hour, Jill had had enough and led him out, promising they'd come back another day.

They returned to her flat and spent what was left of the afternoon in bed. He announced that he'd be going home that night and she didn't try and dissuade him. There was still a limit, which both recognised, to how long they could be at ease in each other's company.

As he was going, she said, 'Tell you what, why don't we meet for tea somewhere tomorrow? Somewhere in town then you aren't doing all the travelling.'

'Yes,' he said, amused and pleased by the idea. He'd never met anyone for tea before. They settled on Piccadilly Circus at four o'clock.

Going back by tube – his car was still dodgy and negotiations with Yvonne for a new one were still incomplete – he was aware of five other people beside himself on the darkened platform. Two of them were couples; the other a solitary man who stood with his hands in his pockets and shoulders hunched. A train

200

came and Harry and the solitary man got into different compartments. Harry's compartment had only two other inhabitants. One was a priest; the other a black man who was reading a magazine. At the next station three youths got in and sat smoking despite the No Smoking sign. After that the carriage stayed reasonably full till Harry himself disembarked. Along the platform about half-a-dozen other people had done the same. Of these, two were women and four men, though at least one of the men looked too old to be a potential assailant. They came together in a small group at the ticket barrier, then went through into the streets beyond. Harry lingered at the back of the group till he was sure no-one was showing any interest in him, then he walked briskly homewards.

The attack came at three o'clock in the afternoon. It was the next day, a peaceful Sunday. His thoughts had been on his coming meeting with Jill so that he hadn't noticed the figure following him down to the deserted platform till it was a split second away from being too late and the blade of the knife was thrusting into him.

He managed to deflect the blow by swinging his arm across it but the blade caught him a deep gash to the fore-arm, cutting to the bone. He jumped backwards and crouched, on guard now and able to take a look at the man behind the knife.

Alex Stone was stocky and thick-necked, with a round, close-cropped head and small moustache. He didn't seem dismayed by the failure of his initial rush but grinned slightly and moved forward, knife at the ready. Harry edged away, though he knew he hadn't far to go before the end of the platform would stop him.

He made a feint as though to grab at the knife, then swung a foot at it instead but Stone, too clever to be caught by that, had stepped back and Harry made contact only with empty air.

They squared up to one another again. Stone jabbed forward with the knife – just testing, not serious – and Harry moved easily away. Then another, more serious slash towards the head. Harry swayed away, then came back quickly in hopeful counter-attack but the other man, light on his feet, had withdrawn and had the knife again in place between them.

There was a train approaching, disturbing the air around them. Both men became aware of it together. The knife-hand faltered but not enough to give Harry his chance, then the train came sweeping past them from its tunnel and, where only a moment ago they'd seemed isolated in space and silence, there was everywhere a rush of noise and movement. It didn't suit Stone. He made a lunge forward so as to force Harry onto his back foot, then turned and ran along the platform to where there was an exit through which he disappeared.

The train doors opened. At the far end two people got off with a child in a pushchair. The guard, hanging from his door, looked at Harry questioningly. Without the time to weigh the pros and cons and knowing only that there was blood crawling down his arm and collecting in his cupped hand, Harry gave a small shake of the head. The doors slid shut and the train pulled away.

There was a new quietness. The disembarked passengers had disappeared so that Harry again had the platform to himself. He also had time to wonder what kind of suicidal stubbornness had made him stay and face his assailant rather than taking the safe way out the train had offered.

He'd also be late for Jill. Very late indeed if he couldn't now get the drop on the murderous Mr Stone.

His arm was bleeding steadily but didn't hurt much. He flexed his hand experimentally. It seemed all right so he decided to ignore the bleeding.

He went along to the gap through which Stone had disappeared. It admitted him to an open area; at one end were the escalators, down the two sides were a number of openings onto the parallel east- and west-bound platforms. A small maze into which Stone had vanished. He could, of course, have high-tailed it up the escalators but Harry couldn't see him leaving the job unfinished.

He moved cautiously across and through onto the other platform. No sign of Mr Stone. There were three youths at the far end, absorbed in their own activities. Harry crossed back to the west-bound platform. Which was still empty.

There was, though – he could have sworn – the faint shuffle of movement somewhere ahead of him, as if someone were leading him on, keeping just out of sight.

He came back to the area between the two platforms. He had to find a way of ending the stalemate, one that would give him the advantage, before Stone found the moment that favoured him. A middle-aged woman came down the escalator. Harry turned so that his bleeding arm was away from her and pretended to be studying a map on the wall. The woman turned onto the east-bound platform. As she did so, she looked this way and that. And her expression changed to one of alarm.

She'd seen Stone; there was no other explanation. And the direction of her gaze allowed Harry to pinpoint exactly where he was hiding.

It was a split-second advantage he couldn't afford to throw away. He took a breath and hurled himself through the opening. On the other side Stone was spreadeagled against the wall. Before he could react to Harry's sudden appearance, Harry had hold of the hand with the knife, then slammed his body into Stone, winding him. The knife clattered to the floor. Harry caught it with his foot and sent it skidding across the platform and down between the rails.

The middle-aged woman gave a short scream and put her hands to her head. Harry stepped away from Stone and threw a blow at his head that caught him above the ear. A second landed on his collar-bone, but the third, when he'd now got the range, lacked the power to put him down. The wound in his arm was taking its toll, weakening him.

Stone had ducked away. He looked at Harry advancing towards him; there was a moment of indecision, then Stone stepped to the platform's edge and dropped down between the rails.

It took him beyond the reach of Harry who could only stand and watch, aware now of other people appearing on the platform and of shouts and screams. Stone was crouching down and fumbling for the weapon. There was the sound of an approaching train.

Stone heard it and looked up. A pair of twin headlights were making their wavering approach down the tunnel.

There were shouts warning Stone of the train and of the live rail to which he was perilously close. Even Harry found himself adding to the chorus. The danger he'd face if Stone emerged with the knife was submerged by the urgency of the moment.

Stone had finally got a grip on the knife and was moving slowly and carefully to avoid the live rail, too slowly and too carefully it seemed for the train was almost upon him.

There was a screeching of brakes that drowned the screams of the watchers. Now clear of the live rail, Stone crouched down then made an almighty spring that carried him across the very face of the train and onto the platform where he landed full-length.

Harry knew he must tackle him immediately. Though for a moment he, like everyone else, was rendered immobile by the sheer closeness of the escape. By that and by his growing sense of weakness and sickliness.

Stone turned, looking for him. When he saw him, there was a look of triumph on his face. He started to rise. Harry tensed himself, trying to summon up his failing energies. Till he saw that Stone was not rising but had fallen back and that his look of triumph had turned to puzzlement.

There were renewed screams as they could now all see how his desperate leap to safety had taken him clear of the train. and the live rail only to bring him down onto the blade of his own knife.

XV

There followed a period of near-hysteria, that subsided to mere confusion, over which order was quickly restored. Railway staff, policemen and ambulancemen arrived at the double, trains were stopped and gawping passengers held at bay. In the midst of it all, Harry sat and nursed his wounded arm, and Alex Stone breathed his last even before they'd got him tied to a stretcher.

Another stretcher came for Harry but he refused it and rode the escalator to the surface where a policeman got into the back of an ambulance with him.

As his wound was dressed, he thought about Jill and asked whether a message could be got to her. He also began to wonder, seeing the policeman sticking doggedly by his side as he was processed through Casualty, what would happen now and whether he might not end up carrying the can for everybody.

A detective in plain clothes arrived. He was polite and formal and asked Harry for his account of what'd happened. It was clear from the outset he'd already spoken to other witnesses – in particular to the middle-aged woman who'd come down the escalator and seen the whole of the final tussle. It was a relief to Harry to find he was being treated as a near-victim rather than as a potential perpetrator of the crime and that there was no doubt but that the knife had been Stone's own and his death accidental.

Taking his cue from this, Harry told how he'd been on his way to meet his girl-friend when suddenly, hey presto, there'd been this knife-wielding maniac demanding money; he'd resisted and been cut, and then the train had come along to buy him a brief respite before battle had been rejoined. That he might have known his attacker previously or that Stone's motive might have been anything other than a straightforward mugging didn't seem to occur to anyone; and Harry saw no reason to enlighten them.

'And how're you feeling now?' asked the detective cheerfully when he'd got his statement.

'Oh, not too bad. Though I don't intend making a habit of this.'

'You're going to be something of a hero, you know.'

'Who is?'

'You. Fighting off a mugger like that. The newspaper boys are going to love it.'

It was an unwelcome thought. Besides Harry's natural antipathy to seeing his mug splashed across the dailies, there was always the possibility that such publicity might yet link him with the dead man and prompt the police into further investigation.

'I don't have to talk to 'em though, do I?'

'Not if you can avoid it.'

'There must be a back door to this place. Can't you let me out that way?'

In the end he got his way, left through a staff entrance at the rear of the hospital and caught a passing taxi. Trying to sort out his priorities, he decided that, number one, he had to find Jill and, number two, he had to find somewhere to hide away till the fuss had died down.

Both of which were achieved within the hour. He traced Jill back to her flat where, alerted by the police to something of what had happened, she was waiting anxiously for news of him. Having heard his story, she insisted he stayed. She would nurse him; he would be

207

out of the eye of the press: what could be better?

He spoke to Yvonne by phone the following morning, knowing he had to reach her before the police or press did. He told her he was at Jill's flat and had been hurt in a fight with Stone.

She said, 'I had a feeling there was something awful going to happen.'

'Well, it did. But fortunately it happened to him.' And he told her the manner of Stone's death. Then he said, 'The police have got the idea I didn't know Stone from Adam. Which is what I want 'em to think. 'Cause if they ever start thinking otherwise then they're not going to be happy till they've got the whole story. And you know what that'll mean.'

There was a moment's silence as she considered it.

'Who else might connect you with Stone?'

'Only Phil Holliday and friends. And they aren't likely to go broadcasting it,' said Harry, who'd now had time to think things through. 'And Graham Bonnington-Price.'

'Who?'

'Never mind. I can square it with him. But I mean you do realise what I'm asking you to do . . .?'

'Well, I don't know what the legal term would be, but it sounds to me like you're asking me to help you cover up murder, blackmail and robbery.'

'Something like that, yes.'

'I don't know that Clifford would have approved.' He held his breath, wondering whether she was joking. Then she said, 'Mind you, we do guarantee complete confidentiality so I don't suppose I've much choice, have I?' And he knew it was all right: she was going to play along.

'Thanks. Now I suppose I'd better ring Phil Holliday and let him in on the act.'

'When you do, tell him he can expect his bill. It's time somebody paid for all this.'

By the end of the week it seemed to Harry that they'd got away with it. The press made what they could of the story but were short on hard facts and pictures. The role of Harry the hero remained in some doubt: hadn't the mugger fallen on his own knife in some kind of bizarre accident? So that Harry escaped the full treatment.

Only at the inquest did he have to emerge and face the flash-bulbs but by that time the story was going cold and had been relegated to the inside pages. Nor was the coroner's verdict of misadventure one to grab the headlines.

His arm was healing nicely and things returning to normal, save that he was still resident in Jill's flat.

'I ought to kick you out,' she said. 'Now you're not at death's door any more.'

'I'm still convalescing.'

'Is that what you call it? Anyway, it's up to you. But don't think I'll be offended if you decide to leave.'

He thought about it and, unable to decide what to do for the best, was still there a week later. On the day they took the stitches out of his wound Jill suggested they celebrate so he bought tickets for the RSC production of *Macbeth* at the Barbican.

'Are you sure that's what you want to do?' she asked, surprised at his choice.

'Yes,' he said defiantly. 'Why, aren't they any good?'

'Oh, they're not bad. I just didn't know you were keen on Shakespeare.'

'I'll try anything once.'

In the event he enjoyed it more than the other play they'd seen together. It wasn't just that he felt less self-conscious about being at the theatre in Jill's company. The play itself was the stuff of murder and violence that struck him as being not too far from home, if you overlooked the funny costumes. He felt sorry for Macbeth, a man honoured by his country for valour in the field then led up the garden path by a gang of deceitful witches and a pushy wife.

For Jill, too, the play seemed to have struck a familiar chord.

'You know when Macbeth says I am in blood stepped in so far that should I wade no more . . . Well, I can't quote any more, but basically he's saying that he's up to his neck in violence whichever way he turns. You remember that bit?'

'No.'

'Well, it made me think of you.'

He laughed, then saw she was serious and unsmiling.

'Why me?'

'Oh, just . . . you're not so deeply involved with all these villains that you can never escape from them, are you?'

'I thought I'd escaped already.'

She looked at him a moment, then shook her head as if regretting her words.

'Sorry,' she said. 'It's just me being silly.'

Was it though? he wondered, struck by what she'd said. Could he really shed his former life like an old skin or would there always be something left over from it and waiting to surprise him?

He might well have thought so had he known of the surprise to come.

He'd by now gone back to working from the office, judging that neither police nor press had any further interest in Stone's death. His habit was to start each day by completing the previous day's reports, so that he was at his desk when Yvonne announced there was Phil Holliday on the phone wanting to speak to him.

Puzzled, he lifted the receiver.

'Phil?'

'Harry, it's come. It's here.'

'What is?'

'Another letter.'

He must have misheard.

'Another what?'

'Another letter. Another one of them blackmail letters. Telling me to get the money together and everything.'

It couldn't be. Alex Stone was dead and buried. The case was closed. They'd had a cheque from Phil Holliday in payment for their services and very grateful he'd been too.

'I don't believe it.'

'Neither did I, mate. But it's here, I can promise you.'

'When did it arrive?'

'This morning. In the post. It's the same sort of envelope as the first one, same sort of paper and everything. Harry, what is this? I thought it was all finished. I thought you'd promised me you'd got it sorted!'

'Are you at the shop now?'

'Yes. Daren't go anywhere else, dare I?'

'I'll be there in ten minutes.'

Arriving at the shop, he was taken by Phil into the back room. Then there it was, being held out for him to inspect – similar envelope, paper and type-face as before. The postmark was local and yesterday.

'What're you going to do, Harry? You've got to do something.'

'Well, let me read it first.'

'Dear Mr Holliday,' said the letter, 'The time has come for payment. I want the ten thousand pounds in used ten- and twenty-pound notes. Make them into a parcel and place that parcel in the left-luggage locker at

King's Cross Station. Then keep the key of the left-luggage locker. I shall be communicating with you again to tell you where to send it. I should also warn you that I have been aware of your attempts to trace me and will tolerate them no longer. Be wise, Mr Holliday, do as I say and you will never hear from me again. You have one week from today in which to place the money in the locker.'

Harry read it twice, then passed it back to him.

'Well?'

'Can you raise it?'

Phil stared. 'You think I should? I mean come on, Harry, is that what you're saying? After all I've paid you, you're telling me there's nothing you can do?'

Harry shrugged. It was what he felt like saying, certainly. This was a case he'd already solved and put behind him. Now here it was, come back to life in cruel mockery of all his efforts. He felt helpless, literally clueless.

'There must be something you can do,' urged Phil.

'What?'

'How the hell should I know?'

'I told you at the start I wasn't making any promises. I'm not the Old Bill. I can't watch left-luggage lockers day and night.'

'But you can't just walk away, Harry. Not now.'

Why couldn't he? He'd risked his neck on Phil's behalf and owed him nothing. Nor did Phil any longer owe the agency.

'Please, Harry.'

'Give me a day or two to think about it,' said Harry, reluctant to abandon the other man without giving him something to cling to. 'I'll give you a ring.'

He returned to the office and told Yvonne what'd happened. She was as surprised as he'd been and had no more idea of what further help they might be.

212

'You've done everything you could. I mean he can't expect miracles.'

'Try telling him that.'

In truth, though, it wasn't only Phil Holliday's resentment that irked him. Harry had been secretly proud of having brought the case to a satisfactory conclusion, albeit a bloody one. Now the second letter had turned his whole investigation into a piece of futile self-deception. He felt angry and obscurely betrayed at the way his success had topsy-turvied into failure.

'I mean, face it,' he said to Yvonne. 'I hadn't any evidence – anything at all – to tie Stone in with the blackmail letters.'

'So why did he try and kill you?'

'Well, I don't know. But I do know this – the man had been in prison almost from the day of the robbery till now. So why should he want to go blackmailing anybody? He still had his share of the loot. Some fifty-odd thousand quid. I mean one thing you don't do in the nick – you don't spend a lot.'

'You've done everything you could,' repeated Yvonne quietly. 'If he wants any more he'll just have to go to the police.'

'He can't go to the police.'

'Well, that's not our fault, is it?'

'No,' said Harry abruptly, still unable to free himself from the feeling that it was.

He sat alone in his office and tried to think. All right, so Stone wasn't the blackmailer. He had the cast-iron alibi of being six feet under on the day the second letter was sent. What then had he had to fear from Harry's investigations? Why had he tried to kill him? Intriguing question to which he'd no answer.

And what about the other robbers, those who were neither dead nor in jail and were therefore candidates for sending blackmail letters and collecting from left-

213

luggage lockers? He thought of Ronnie Franks, selling second-hand cars. Neil Patterson, into Glaswegian boy-friends and antiques. Tommy Coyle and his life plagued by dogs. Frank Metcalf, with his pub and his heavy friends. It wasn't a long list, only four out of the original nine. Of the other five, Les Pinfield, Vince Jardine and Alex Stone were dead, Maurice Scanlon in jail, and Phil Holliday trying to raise ten thousand quid. Was it, then, someone else altogether, someone who hadn't taken part in the robbery but who knew enough about it to be a threat to those who had?

Another point. The second letter referred to Phil Holliday's attempts to trace his blackmailer. That is, to Harry's own efforts on Phil's behalf. So whoever had written it knew Phil had employed him.

Taking a sheet of paper, Harry drew up a list of names. On it was everyone to whom he'd ever spoken about the Phil Holliday case, no matter who, no matter when.

Then he began crossing names off. Either because they couldn't have known enough to have embarked on blackmail or because, for a variety of other reasons, they were in no position to do so.

It left him with a single name.

Taking with him the sheet of paper, and the single name, he emerged from the office. Yvonne looked at him anxiously.

'There's somebody I want to see,' he said. 'Shan't be long.'

'About the blackmail letters?'

'Yes.'

'You know who's been sending them?'

He hesitated.

'I'll tell you when I get back.'

214

XVI

Since his last visit the garden had been cut back in anticipation of winter, its bushes pruned and plants moved indoors. Everything about the outside of the house was as spic and span as before, the paintwork looking newly washed and the drive swept clean.

Paula Pinfield, widow of Les, answered the door wearing a pink trouser-suit and gold sandals. Insofar as she'd ever been in mourning at all, she was now clearly out of it. She looked at Harry in surprise.

'Mrs Pinfield,' he said. 'It's Harry Sommers. You remember I called to see you before . . .?'

'Yes.'

'Can I come in?'

She gave a small shrug, as if to say why not, then stood back and waved a red-tipped hand.

'Thanks,' said Harry, and stepped past her into the house.

'Is this to do with Les?' she asked, following him into the lounge.

'I suppose it is, yes.'

'Sit down.'

'Thanks.'

'Are you still working for Phil Holliday?'

'Not for much longer. See, I think I've just about found what he wanted to know.'

'Who was sending the letters?'

'Yes.'

If she was rattled, it wasn't showing. She lit a

cigarette and perched on the edge of the sofa, offering Harry a fixed smile which said that she hadn't a clue what this was all about but was willing enough to listen. He knew he was skating on thin ice. Unless he could draw at least the first flicker of a response from her then he'd be through it and sinking fast.

'You know what happened to Alex Stone, do you?'

'Who?'

'The man who killed your husband.'

'But I don't know who killed my husband.'

'Oh, I think you do, Mrs Pinfield. I know I do anyway.'

She went through a small pantomime of surprise and shock.

'You can't be serious.'

'Why not? What else can you be about a murder?'

Her tone changed, hardening.

'I think you'd better get to the point.'

'The point is that Alex Stone killed your husband.'

'And have you told the police this?'

'Not yet.'

'And why ever not? Since you seem so sure.'

'Because there doesn't seem to be a lot of point. Not now that Alex Stone's dead. You knew that, did you?'

She hesitated. Yes, he thought, you knew all right.

'I think I might have read somewhere . . .'

'I think you might. Well, Stone was the ninth robber.'

'Pardon?'

'Alex Stone. Was robber number nine. For which your Les got into a lot of bother.'

'Mr Sommers, I really don't know what you're talking about.'

'Oh, I think you do,' said Harry, hoping to God he was right. 'I think you'd made it your business to know everything about what Les was getting up to.'

216

'Mr Sommers, I don't know why you've come back here, but I have to say that I don't much care for the attitude you seem to be taking.'

'I'm sorry about that.'

'Now will you please explain yourself or leave.'

'Oh, I'll explain all right,' said Harry, 'though I think you probably know it all anyway. See, after the Fleet Television robbery, Les was supposed to have Alex Stone bumped off.'

'I hope you know what you're saying.'

Harry ignored that and continued. 'But he didn't. Instead, he told Stone what was going on. Told him how the other members of the gang wanted him killed. And so Stone high-tailed it for Australia. Right?'

'I don't know what you're talking about.'

'Oh, I think you do.'

'Mr Sommers, I'm getting very tired of this.'

'I'm sorry. I'll be quick.'

'I think I'd rather you didn't bother at all.'

Harry ignored her again. 'Like I say, Les tipped him off and Stone disappeared to Australia. Only there was something else as well. Some financial deal between the two of them. I don't know the details but, whatever they were, it meant Les was left holding Stone's money. And then, lo and behold, Stone's barely set foot in Australia before he's sent down for seven years. Which makes everything hunky-dory for Les.'

'If you're so certain about all this, then why come and tell me? Why not go to the police?'

'Maybe I'm going to. Maybe I'm on my way now and I've just stopped off here to tell you first.'

She said nothing, just tapped the ash from the end of her cigarette into an ashtray shaped like a racing-car. There was a new hesitancy about her that encouraged Harry to think he was, after all, on the right track.

'Only even jail sentences come to an end sooner or

217

later. And, once Stone is out, the first thing he wants to know is what's happened to his money. And when he can't get a reply all the way from sunny Australia, he comes back over here looking for it. Which was when Les started to get really worried.'

'I hope you've got some evidence for these ridiculous accusations.'

'Bags of it,' said Harry, then went on quickly before she could ask what it was: 'Because, of course, Les had spent the money by then, hadn't he? Spent his own and spent Stone's as well.'

'Really.'

'Well, you're the one who told me how he could never hang on to money. How he was a gambler. And not the sort that wins either.'

'I think perhaps you're a gambler as well, Mr Sommers.'

'Only on certainties.'

There was another pause, which Harry allowed to lengthen. She wanted to find out how much he knew before deciding which way to jump. But he'd learned a lot about this interrogation lark since their last encounter. What mattered wasn't how much he knew but how much she didn't.

'So you're saying that this man killed Les,' she said finally.

'Yes.'

'Did he tell you that?'

'As good as. You know he had a go at me?'

'I read something about it.'

'Speaks for itself then, doesn't it? He was out to do for me because of what I'd found out about him.'

'So why didn't you tell that to the police? From what I read in the newspapers, you said you'd never set eyes on him before.'

'Because I'd one or two loose ends to tie up first.

Which you very kindly did for me when you sent Phil Holliday that second letter.'

She turned slowly till she was staring him full in the face.

'I don't think I heard that.'

'Oh, I think you did.'

'You're accusing me of sending those blackmail letters?'

'Yes.'

'One of which – as I'm sure I don't need to remind you – was to my own husband?'

'Yes.'

'Then all I can say is that that's the most wicked, nasty, vile thing I've ever heard.'

'Mrs Pinfield,' said Harry evenly, 'I'm not working for the Old Bill. I'm working for Phil Holliday, who asked me to find out who was blackmailing him. So we can settle it now if you like, between the two of us. If we don't – well then, I'll pass it on and it'll be out of my hands.'

'I think you've got the most amazing bloody cheek,' she said, standing. 'And, what's more, I think you're off your head and if you think I'm going to listen to any more of this then you're wrong. So you can just get out of here, go on!'

He stood up, though he knew that if he left without the truth then there'd be little point in returning to look for it.

'I don't think you're being very wise.'

'Oh, am I not?' she flung back at him. 'We'll see who's being wise, shall we? Because, Mr Private Detective, I know people who're going to get rather annoyed when they hear what you've been saying to me. I know people who're going to make you sorry for even thinking it.'

Now the chips were down and the housewifely

veneer thrown over, she looked liable to attack him herself.

'Go on, get out of this house!'

He took a step towards the door but kept on talking.

'And I know people who won't be too happy about what you're doing, Mrs Pinfield. Frank Metcalf and Neil Patterson for example. They aren't going to like it one little bit when they hear what you're up to.'

'You just keep your mouth shut about me!'

'No,' said Harry firmly. 'You want me to go – I'll go. But if I do, then I can promise you now – everybody that was on that job is going to know you're threatening to blow the whistle on them.'

She opened her mouth, then hesitated and closed it again and he knew he'd got through to her. She might still want to kill him, but mention of Les's old mates had reminded her of a world she understood all too well and where retribution was short and swift, Old Testament stuff. It scared her where talk about the police had left her cold.

'You wrote the letters,' said Harry. 'All three of them.'

'What, and blackmail my own husband . . .?' she protested, but now it was without conviction, a despairing bluster.

'No. It was only after Les was killed that you saw how you were fixed. Left alone with no money, 'cept for the launderette business that you're not exactly keen on. And, since it was on account of the robbery that Les had been killed, you thought about that and how you could take a rake-off from it.'

'You can't prove anything.'

'I don't have to. Sit down.'

She did. Just lowered herself down onto the sofa, all the fight gone out of her.

'You typed the first letter, the one to Les, and then

you showed it to Phil and told him it'd arrived before Les had been killed. Then you sent the second letter to Phil. Didn't you?'

She muttered something he couldn't hear.

'What?'

'I deserved it. The money. I deserved something after all them years. Something more than a bleeding launderette!'

'Perhaps you did,' he said quietly, able to soft-pedal now she'd told him what he wanted.

'All that money he'd had and wasted.'

'What about Alex Stone? Did he have Stone's money as well?'

She nodded.

'Why?'

'It was like you said. Les warned him that the others were out to get him and that his best bet was to leave the country.'

'But he couldn't take the money with him?'

'Not then, no. Not when the robbery was still big news. So Les was going to look after it, then send it on.'

As the last pieces fell into place, the picture became clear.

'But Les got greedy, did he? He wanted Stone's share as well?'

She nodded. She looked suddenly older and vulnerable so that he felt almost sorry for her, seeing the desperation that'd led her to act as she had.

'It was when he heard about Stone being sent down.'

'I see.'

'I told him he was a fool but . . . well, first of all, he was just going to borrow from it. Just needed a few hundred for this or that. And then it'd all gone, and next thing he knew Stone was out and Les was scared . . . too scared to know what to do.'

For a moment Harry thought she was in tears, but no,

her eyes were dry. It was more anger, not sorrow for her dead husband but bitterness at how she herself had been left high and dry. The little sympathy he'd felt evaporated. She'd had her share of the money, no doubt; then had schemed to twist her husband's murder into bringing her more.

'So Stone came back over here to collect his share from Les and found it'd all gone,' said Harry.

'Yes.'

'And so he killed him.'

'Yes.'

'But, rather than tell the police what you knew, you decided it'd be more profitable if you kept it to yourself and used it to screw money out of Phil Holliday.'

She looked at him, her eyes blazing.

'Get out.'

'In a minute. Just so long as you understand that your little game's over. There won't be any more letters, will there?'

'I'll get you for this,' she said. 'One day, I swear I will.'

It was as near to an admission of defeat as he was going to get. He smiled and stood up.

'I'll tell Phil he's no more to worry about. There's no need for anybody else to know. It can be our little secret.'

She let loose with a mouthful of obscenities.

'I'll see myself out,' said Harry, and did so quickly.

He explained it all to Jill that night. He knew mention of the case alarmed her with its harking back to his violent past but he couldn't resist telling her of his triumph. She was suitably impressed and pleased, though perhaps as much at its now being all over as at his ingenuity in solving it.

'But how did you know it was her?' she asked.

'I didn't know. Just that I had to do something and she seemed the best bet.'

'Why?'

'Well, whoever had sent that last letter knew both about the original robbery and about my investigations. So there weren't that many people it could have been.'

'There was me. I knew about both.'

'Yes, I thought of you.'

'Oh, thanks . . .!'

'But then we went to see *Macbeth*.'

Baffled, she said, 'And . . .?'

'Well, that reminded me that behind every successful villain there's a wife waiting to spend every penny she can lay her hands on.'

'Oh, I see,' she laughed. 'So it's all down to Lady Macbeth, is it?'

He nodded. 'Can be useful sometimes, a bit of culture.'

'I'm glad I've helped.'

'You have,' he said. 'In more ways than one.'

She'd come into his life at a strange time, when Clifford Humphries's death had catapulted him into the role of private eye. Then he'd nearly made a botch of everything, beating up her husband and being almost knifed by Alex Stone.

Her question still haunted him: would he be able to turn his back on his past and its villainous associates? Without her, probably not. With her, he felt he had a fighting chance.

If you have enjoyed this book and would like to receive details of other Walker Adventure titles, please write to:

Adventure Editor
Walker and Company
720 Fifth Avenue
New York, NY 10019